THESE SPELLS

THESE
SPELLS

John Hownam

Matador
9 Priory Business Park,
Wistow Road, Kibworth Beauchamp,
Leicestershire. LE8 0RX
Tel: 0116 279 2299
Email: books@troubador.co.uk
Web: www.troubador.co.uk/matador
Twitter: @matadorbooks

ISBN 978 1789016 734

British Library Cataloguing in Publication Data.
A catalogue record for this book is available from the British Library.

Printed on FSC accredited paper
Printed and bound in Great Britain by 4edge Limited
Typeset in 11pt Aldine401BT by Troubador Publishing Ltd, Leicester, UK

Matador is an imprint of Troubador Publishing Ltd

For Gail

And so –

All the webs are broken, each little globe circumference lost – reflections dropped and scattered upon this soil of a zillion dreams – and then some.

Alas, all mouths are open; those fallen dead and reborn; watching spiders weave and spin, thirsting for those pearls stretched across your skin.

So far away we were, eager and sparkling and darting between here and there; in a hole behind a star, beneath other woods where, undiscovered, we were far, too far away.

Away and away, beyond the final stone of the final city of the final day – built to remain as a marker; end of the beginning, hear the bell ringing, the choir roll, and the rook resting upon his cornerstone, gathering leaves and bones and dead things caught up in the changing wind. For such is the way of corners and doorways: to gather together those last bits of forever.

Unlike this loop of unspooling time.

This filigree of form that turns out and toward.

Blooms like blood behind you. Breathe in and blow it away. Breathe out black to grey.

The trees are dressed and fragmented in that breathing out and coming in of sunshine. Between the branches where light catches and picks strange puzzles. I see you drawing hearts on the ground, where the leaves have not fallen yet.

Tilt your head and pull a sigh. Make a word. Make a wish. And thirdly, draw a line and cross it – for now the world is changed and forever your evers will be gains and your dreams unhooked from those crooked branches.

But see how it chaffs, how it runs raggedly away, and the fray and the threads that embroider every shred of vision aspiring love and tall towers and roses festooned for all beautiful and bright this dazed light caught capturing trees in a breeze. Dance with the moment, but let it go – for all your tattered roses and branches and wishes and tolls were sufficient payment, no doubt.

And now, forget all these things, merely words, nothing more. Forget all the images stacked up so tall they would fall. Forget and forget and let it all go – for, whatever your wishes there is no more to know. And there is no more to tell.

But you hoped, nonetheless, in a hidden heart there would be a space, some forbidden place, some hideaway knoll into which you could crawl and draw the undergrowth up over your head and kick in your heels, the remains of the dead who lie undisturbed, asleep in their webs.

Stay then. What will it matter? What design to whatever purpose you incline? Stay – buried deep – snagging those beds.

However, let us pull back that dreamy veil, frail and refracted, elegantly distracted, dazzled and July green.

Then wait until dawn, watch night slip alone, loosened from its slipknot tethers. And whether or never or whenever or not you decide to slip and tiredly drop, tighten the rope that tightens us together and strengthen the day that will bring us forever to a moment, but nothing more.

Stop!

Stop!

This is far and far enough. Just raise a glass and a cheer to a chance that, out of nothing, we were rushed here, beguiled and bereft.

And if the wine should find thee, perhaps in that hole behind that star; sip from the moments that lustre, wet lips to thrust her, dancing against the dark. This is how it all begins and begins and begins again. And this is how it sends thee, dithering and lost away.

The broken hearts fall into line, speechless and motionless, yet beautifully divine. The indented display and foolish hoorays of lost and new beginnings. Come gather and collect, better to forget than allow those dreams a tether. Let them all go. Watch just how slow they rise and mingle and sever. Pull back your breath and let your breath go. Watch how it blusters away, so quickly and so empty, so nothing-to-nothing, so blacker than black into grey.

Hence here we divide. All our sorrows untied. All our breaths and deaths, loves and lies, broken by…a dream and moment's hesitation.

There is nothing to say and nothing to add; nothing to show or frame or say we have had. Here lies the moment. Let it rest in peace. We must stand in silence and remember this. Let us cross our hearts and hope to die, let us whisper a prayer and close our eyes. Let us go. Let it go. Let it dissolve away. For another day will dawn and another summer be born, and the endless nights cradle us weeping at the moon.

I think this should end here. This is where all words run out. This is where the spirit splutters and stutters devout. This is where it all ends. Just one more line and a dot to say we have finished, tied and tarred the knot. It has gone – gone – gone away.

Wave upon wave upon wave set in motion, rising beneath and below. From sail unto sail, beyond a swell and hollow that catches us to hold us a time. May gaze into our eyes seeking a sign to seek explanation, only a blotted destination – ink imbrued upon darkness.

Upwards and downwards, sideways and in; we twist and we turn, unfold out within; we rally then flounder, bigger and louder, rolling away again. Rocks rumbling, tumbling and gone.

Then I am back into dark and it is all far away, and this moment I live in begs just to stay and share and spare some fraction of time, split it into slithers, laid in a line. We follow it on, along and forever, endlessly, heedlessly, pointlessly, but never arriving or leaving, remaining instead – hearing those rocks rolling ahead. And as we close upon the day, we recede, retracing our steps, hunkered down low, exchanging short breaths, for there is nothing to know, and nothing to be given.

Then silence as the lateness sets in. Senselessly smothering the skin, a membrane dividing twilights sliding and riding upon a blood red horse. Hooves raised, mane flayed, sprayed, like snakes between the stars. We can measure this weather, temperate together, and wait until we are redeemed; or we can cancel and wait, although it is late, wondering as shadows cross.

And as the poles align to the midnight chime and the clocks tick between pauses, we close our eyes and imagine the skies flooding teams of horses. They pull and they steer, without fear. They sweep and wreck unaware. They fade against a spattered universe, galaxies out.

You see.

There is a moment between things, threaded weightlessly upon the periphery of vision, that sees without eyes, thinks without thought, and dreams whilst some drift among the living. This moment is an unhappening. This unhappening a journey toward away, turns to return and fades all that we ever believed in.

If you thought you might wake or your eyes about to open, consider the undoing and unhappening of it all. Consider the moment – hanging there – on the periphery of vision. For what, or whom, does it await? Unthinking a thought, or a thought we thought to commence. And why dawdle and dither when death is yet nearer, for the living have nothing to see.

Come away from it all. This derangement. This madness. When our moment slips like a breath between the sheets. Can't you hear it? Feel its weightlessness unravelling time? Undoing it all! Can't you feel yourself loosened free as the clock hand advances, and the oceans of a trillion, trillion, trillion souls push with all their might, but do not say a word, nor dare a whisper – or ever open their eyes?

But by and by that fragility will gently withdraw. Barely noticed, but for the darkness that remains circled and spiralled around you.

M ark the dawn. The webs that were broken are, once again, repaired, reborn and stretched eight-finger tight. Pulled and disjointed to snare, transparent lairs. Seems we are already caught in these corners of our own - and unable to find our way home.

Where are we, sweetest? Have we not counted the stars? Have we not counted them together and matched our scores? Where are we now? Are we truly lost?

And if I pull you close, tell you not to fear, a ghost whispers into your ear.....hesitates.

And a light burns brightly, burns holes into my eyes and the stars the holes hide pull me wider - and I realise the finality of this, this forever without you; this endless moment of moments, hoping that there, out there, upon the periphery of my vision, you will quietly wait.

Please forgive me this madness. I speak but hear no words. I beg but my lips never move. I look, but only through the lids of my eyes, and I breathe and feel my chest rise and I know I am alive, and I *know* you are in the land of faraway webs and holes and stars and vague, very vague peripheries.

Oh – dear – God.

It is as if I awaken, but never for long. For as sure as the world lightens it all turns wrong and I see you as clear as day. You are smiling – and still dressed cotton white.

"Take me with you," I say.

"Then come, take my hand."

"Reach a little closer. You are too far away."

"Open your eyes."

"I do not know how. Where are you?"

There is a spark. All else radiates away and the sun and the moon and the stars all sliver like silver and quicksilver away. And there comes upon destiny this something unexplained; encapsulates and perambulates, but is unable to change.

From.….here – caught between rushing trains and platforms and stations without names. No windows, no tickets. This is indeed tangled in deed.

Chased then embraced following a thousand storms, this metamorphic butterfly of shadowy forms lifts upon a thermal high above the webs, above the currents, an occurrence that might have left us for dead.

Deader than dead, heads turned aside, as lost and forgotten, dust will decide, and dust shall be blown and gusted and scattered and pushed there and shattered like glass upon rocks.

Oh, here then we are, below those webs. Something tells me those heads need look back, for their way and decay are truly lost. And there is no further thought unto this dust which, already scattered, has blown across the plains and otherly terrains.

And again we shall arise – evening fireflies.

And again we shall lift, up and adrift.

Yet again it all turns and turns again.

Every second, minute, every refrain.

Every quark of forever, every breath that has breathed.

Every crossroad we pondered.

Everything we believed.

Infinity squared, anchored and paired, hooked to the root of eternity. A stain on the stars, endless stars that spin in the wheel of uncertainty.

What does it all mean?

Spinning to where?

Am I awake in these dreams?

Will I find you here?

Questions and questions. This is all I have. Other than otherness, senseless bizarre.

I shall still awhile and rest my breathing; because, if I listen, I can hear your dreaming, and you're dreaming I am dreaming of you.

And there you are, dancing on a shore, waves lifting, sun silting, gilting the fine light hair on your arms. And your smile is of laughter, of here and hereafter, and your voice is a pause between creation and cause, full pirouette to a sigh. Wondering why and how I found you here.

You brought me here. I watch this line, so delicate and ultimately finite.

Draw a line and step over it.

Cast a circle and step into it.

Dig a hole and climb under it.

Point to a star and you must follow it.

Lines and circles and holes and stars, this is where we are.

"Is it all making sense yet?"

Shhhhh!

"Okay. Let me explain."

We kissed before a storm in a labyrinth of twists and

shifts between lines undefined. We met beneath a moon, cast shadows like tombstones, slabbed and upright. We met, but left and returned again. Is that how it was? Is that how we remember this? Or is *this* only I?

Perhaps, then, the storm was in fact unborn and not ready yet to tear our world apart. Perhaps, at that, there was no moon either; just another vacuum wherein nothing seemed real anymore. Nothing has *ever* seemed real, but concealed, unrevealed – images that might become some monsterous form we can no longer control.

The storm, actually, *was* about to break. I remember this. The pot bellied clouds lowering upon the earth, and the slices of moonlight – halos ringing in our ears, thunderous and continuous, peals and layers of lightening, prayers calling unto the Almighty. Brightened and lightened. Silhouettes against the sky. You and I - small figures behind the bellows – old cellos – low and deep and dark. That is where we were born.

I fold like some collapsing shape onto the wheel of continuous turning.

And now I am running as reality breaks like waves, that glass against a rock. And I am broken as the nightmare ahead of me stops to block my way. And I know of nowhere else to go.

Garnet red, radiating threads, spokes become webs; woven to break my fall (no surprise at all). How else? Unless I die, released from it all. How else? Unless the envoy be given receipt for the deed of the dead. Let it be said – it is written in the reddest red of red, my soul is not allowed to leave here.

And as the images waltz and curve away, I remain on my own, on my knees, trying to see through the blindness of my eyes. Are you there? Are you hiding in this cryptic muse, tugging clues on the web threads? That I may guess and unravel this various everything?

One more clue, then. Just one more pull on the thread, permeates red against a setting sun. A vibration, a movement to tell me it is done and we can be freed from this separation of souls. As when two horizons meet, the skies sweep clean all edges that they may dance their first dance together. Watched from afar. This will be us as we merge as one, in a space reserved for as long as we can remember.

This is our due, as we as one, too, belong and as deep as deep and as high as high as ever a high may be. It is written in dust and scratched in the rust of a gusting twilight, blustering the sails of the last ships waiting to cross beyond the pale.

Ahh! This is where we are floating – along that edge, that division and collision of horizons dressed to dance.

'Let the music commence' as we embrace, slow moving, my arm around waist. Feel the air move over our skins as the sails blow high and the universe spins. Feel our togetherness jigsawing foreverness. as if everless were never expecting the sway below our feet.

I feel your breath, though I know your breath has gone. A rhythmic motion against my palms, pressed, but calm. We wax and wane as the stars exchange.

Still we dance to leave the world behind. The sails are full of fullness for the world cannot decide. We tilt, bow spilt, running over a myriad altering currents on errands of their own, where anchors drop like rocks onto uncovered, but undiscovered, bones.

Cross our hearts and cross the lines – for now our world has changed. Enough to sail this carousel of infinite horizons – silently unexplained.

And yet I know I am dancing with a ghost, imagined and surreal. You are in my mind, perfectly unreal, and I can see you so unclearly here – in a teardrop reflection. Neither boat, nor sail, nor waltz or veil, behind which a ghost could hide.

Alone.

A lonely place for souls to divide.

Now spectres dart as frightened phantoms from door-to-door, ceiling to floor, disturbed from their lairs, cloaked on the stairs, climbing away. Descending instead to a place for the dead that is dark and impenetrably grey. For, way beyond this diffused light, there are mutters and cries that the night may swallow it all and put out any brightness between the wicked and the blessed - that they may quietly slip into some sweet nothingness.

It would take the breath of a summer to awaken all this, to bluster and discover this. This place for winter, the cold cycles of a short and skeletal phase. No latch to lift, nor window to raise, no ways or exit days.

Spectres are shadows. There are no angels here, wherever *here* is. Only movements and disturbances from those become lost. Like myself.

I look for your face as I would shapes in a fire, making out features like jokers and demons, but searching for reasons why I am unable.

(Because angels don't abide here)

(Because good things never arrive here)

(Because – to be lost translates as unfound)

(And here there is no summer ground)

Scritches and scratches, like lifting those latches, then scurries that flurry to a corner unseen. Thus, beyond the catch of this surreal dream to dither and wait, too late to wither or whether or if ever or not, there are no further clues only states and conditions and a very vague destiny swirling next to me, drawn behind definite lines.

To pull that line forward I would hesitate a pause, breath held, eyes spelled, locked by the jaws of a delayed incision. Yet, evertheless, so we choose that vision, imprisoned behind the holes in our eyes. Because the stars in the skies follow us, not *we* follow *they*. Destinies cast in the loom, woven by whoever the night turns. If it is so, then I suspect we will catch upon the threads – the lines – one beyond the other, collected in circles spidering into the ether and hooked into those curious angles that jangle and vibrate, as we creatures liberate and disturb what was always meant to be.

Not *destiny* – the threads we see sunrayed and splayed tantalising fingers in this penny arcade, where we drop change like they would forever rearrange our lives.

I see all this now, though cryptic it may be. The rhythms of *everything* spectrumed and split, razored ragged and ripped that we may only pursue our line. And, as these cross mine, mis-signed to a line of our own.

So there we go. The stage is set, the end of it – the beginning before the end. It is here we draw the final conclusion, the last remaining illusion, the complete utterness we thought would never shutter us or lock or throw away the key.

Considering this - this optional dance before the kiss; the horizon disguising itself as none of this.

Oh – dear – God.

Enough is enough. The well that was empty now brims to overflowing, soaking and flooding the surrounds that surround and support it.

How is this?

How are we to possibly understand?

What does understanding mean?

E ssentially dazed, ALL is slowly and gradually erased. Every wave minutely delayed, frayed at every edge, broken at every thread, timed, pulled and reformed, whorled into this web.

So, here we are, renewed, then backspaced and deleted again. Broken. Spellbound. Lost and found.

Then I should seek that I might find you. But in seeking know that truly this is a game indeed. I should pray for enlightenment. But every breath of prayer is beyond me. It is enough – such desperate fate. Because, absolutely truly, He might eradicate every last beat of every desperate heart, every end to every start, every love that has been torn and taken apart – Yet, by what? What justice would prevail? An end to all justice, every rule ever written or has so much as troubled a star. 'No more rules'. Seek as you will. It has been disguised, hidden and removed.

What hope?

From afar a moment when I saw you.

Through a dream I heard myself call you.

And I was sure you echoed my call.

But I fell and lost my way.

And I can do nothing if nothing at all. And I slumber and dream, sometimes it seems, gazing beyond those faraway lakes of consiousness.

Sweet somnambulist, she has died and gone, the runner has run.

Come, my sweetheart, that I may gather you up and breathe you back into life. At least brush by my shoulder. *Shhh*! into my ear, soft and smouldered, burning as we unite. Like the horizons we invite to share this coming together. The red sky horses, twilight courses through which every being believes. For if ever a way or end to a day were as final as this, we would see and hear and count the tears behind the stars.

Rectangled and framed, pictured and waned, waxing behind the moon. A storm burrowed too soon into the veins of the night receding. Disappearing and leaving the volumous, fathomless, emptiness of nothing. And silently it hurries away – trying to hide – as if something inside were trying to explain – something.

And the something was, as the something is – a protest against the untogethered. From satanic to platonic, from heaven to forevered, let the angels all sing, let the monsters roar, howling, let the bloodied sing – and the doors to every world open. Every word that was never lost, waiting to be heard. Whispered or mimed, muffled or chimed; absurd, but never crossed.

Wrapped in black. Bleeding into all that. Water coloured, faded into layers, because those unsaid prayers were unable to loosen a thread. And as sure as the dead leave us their beds, the fingers and claws of the beasts that saw us, tighten upon rattled skulls.

So crack my bones and allow me this. Allow me the moment and allow me a wish. For my body endures despite the world, despite the universe, despite it all. My body endures, despite the fact nothing is nothing, neither this, nor that. Nothing is lost and nothing is saved. All the tiny zeros added together suggest we have ways into which we might make something.

There's that *something* again. It falls like a soft rain on your morning window. Runs and chases another along. Watch how they right a wrong and make the universe whole. Make *everything* roll into holes behind stars.

Anyway. That is where we are. This is just how far I can lose my way, and lose you in the process.

I try to remember. You know I do. I try to pull it all together. You know – this thing – me and you. I try and try and wish and believe all this could possibly make us as one – within – this – whateverness.

Yet I have not stopped dancing, imagining you here.

Nor answering if I thought I heard your voice.

I have not stopped remembering.

For it is that alone that pairs our threads.

Connects the two.

Bravely, I assume, the groom presents the bride, the cosmos within which the night resides, the allness around which we freefall and glide like rooks above the cornerstone. For the bride would be the dawn, and the groom receding darkness. And the blades would be drawn, sharp and heartless. And they sickle and sythe cutting back the night which rides the groom away.

I wait here and watch; like a field with a gate wide open. A witness innocent. Imprismed, refracted, distracted by an exactness that would split this into a rainbow wheel. Blades strobe and spin, windmilling, signalling that the end is nigh.

Dear morning.

I shake my head, shake away the hiddeness that rules and dominates this peculiar world and look for a clarity, some polarity that draws and pulls together.

Dear bride, lighten the way.

But I see only the dust from the hooves of the retreating horses.

So be it - I close my eyes, yet they are already closed; squeeze my vision and release the collage – watch them dance and waltz and emerge; yellows, blues and jades, and golds brassy and rolled into emerald and bloody garnet. Watch them fade. Watch the charade, mark it unplayed; cannot yet imagine an end to this dream.

I allow it all to melt into itself. All the hints and riddles and squiggles that sizzle under a scorching sun. Feel the temperature arrow into my flesh, and the infra red bubble below my skin, as our arcing star, closest to earth, ring the bells of midday. She is as high as her right-angled flight will allow, grinning curiously down into the illumination, accumulating her narrow shadows - contrast turned to full on.

And, as the fires and pyres and briars burn, this sun turns a wistful eye to the damp corners, steaming in her heat, where waving and weaving and hazy images meet to arise into higher layers and hold a prayer in remembrance of a storm that has twisted even that all powerful, but mystical, moon and had her chased into the vaults of thunder.

No wonder I wait here, paused in this grand isolation where explanations are laced indecipherable into every line and beaded web. But even now those beads evaporate as our star eradicates even the smallest clue. And the blazing furnaces of hell dry and cure the few ciphers that suggest some hope to pursue.

But I remember.

The moon.

The stars.

The storm about to break.

And a window where I watched your reflection.

Travelling.

I remember the moon most of all.

But still our star is curving across a small sky. She grins because she has a secret of why sometimes we live or die, or both. Dragged-dragging her claws across the blue, ultra-violet, stripping back the heavens set to become host through this eyelet of what might have been.

You were dressed in white.

I can only ever remember you in white.

Late evening drawing her horses into clouds, and chariots to chase. Tasting electricity as we faced out and traced the moon on the glass and raised a wine to the throne of heaven, driving magnificent beasts.

Yet in their wake I pray the Lord my soul to take, for the fires are raging hard. The anvil resounds as our hemisphere surrounds and beats a rhythm of its own.

'It is beautiful,' I said.

And, indeed, born unto the dead we are, and beautiful in as far as red and blue skies merge and stars forecast and predict and spell and spin our destinies. These pulled and knotted where they would appear to be stripped, straightened and aligned. Destiny defined and scripted. Is that not how it was meant to be?

So what of you and me?

'*Come with me,*' you said.

That was then.

And I followed.

But what of all this?

Even now I feel our star moving on. Obliquely as a sun should do. Now pulling and hurrying, for there are other holes to explore and other things to see.

Destiny?

I am not sure.

By and by, as the groom returns, riddles the fire, concerned. Sleep those slices of death. Recalling yet, what was surely about to awaken.

Enough of this. Enough of it all. Whatever is whatever and whenever we default another card turns for another result. Another hand played, every card splayed and fanned for all to see. Is that what I see? Is that all – or not enough? Or is there something hidden? Something beyond the cusp? Another card to turn? Another turn?

Then, explain me this:

If a filament breaks, what is the point of it all?

Broken hearted we die.

Empty and alone we fall.

Helplessly.

Hopelessly we slide.

Like tumbling rocks we roll.

As rocks and blocks into canyons bottomless away, the day is far and lays way beyond the sway of faraway peripheries. And if I am alone, then where are you? How can this be? How can this be true? How can there be no meaning to it all?

Yet I know. I know you are beside me. Even though I cannot see. I do not believe in this ridiculous reverie. You are beside me. This is all I know – as the coldness sets in, and the day decides to slow and shade and fade.

There are fractions of fractions, tiniest subtractions, sparked as if fire from flint, just moments and flickering extractions of a time before now. And a hint of where we were.

How were you dressed?

Why - in white, of course.

There was an aisle and a child (or was that child you?).

There was a mumbling echoed and a humbling before the grace of God.

There were words to be shared.

'You are beautiful,' I said.

'And you are beautifully mine.'

And then a kiss surrendering this, surrounding this dance to begin, this kissing wish to remain and dance forever.

Oh, how obscure.

To see all this, then, then, and then again. To touch all of this and beyond.

Askance our dance and horizons aligned, embraced, graced, we are of a kind, but blinded to the whims of fate and fortune. Too late to tarry and wonder awhile, when the gates are open and the lines run on through and we are wondering and laughing, pondering and laughing – until the laughter runs away. But not this day. For *truly* we are lovers indeed. And the lines feed the rhymes that live and breath and bleed and heed no other essence other than life itself.

But threads and lines and rhymes we follow, for the curfew falls after the morrow and tomorrow's sorrows are not of today's concern. But the lines, nonetheless, carry us and marry us and take us away. And hurry we hurry and hurry on as the blurring distance calls us on. And on still aligned, dancing blinding us to wherever or wherever we are destined or belong.

No signs.

Nothing to align.

We talk, but we mime.

Suspicious of what to believe.

Do not leave me here.

Do not close that door that rises between ceiling and floor. Slammed, sealed, scored by the claws of the beast that has marked this place its own.

I know of no other place.

The beast has grown into a magnificent sky and rolled and made way for the bride.

And as night and day separate the storm, so sun and moon are sworn and a pact made to divide them. The ghosts tarry to watch the sport. The beast rears up from all fours, until, at once, the horses are released.

S o.
    Reset every clock.

Undo every lock.

Return all to their beginnings; everything willing or unwilling to return. Let us restart, reboot and revert entirety unto its singularity. Let us address this at once.

As we watch the storm unfold, slow-motioning, holding onto the latches for fear they might lift and catch us running on. For fear the madness behind it had won and black-inked all the colour away.

"It is beautiful," I said.

Yet the horror this day has been hidden in the folds and creases, between the golden sheets as a ghost whispers:

Reset the clocks.

Reset the clocks.

It is not too late.

Reset the clocks and allow the storm abate, allow the colours to run, seep and jade. Allow the thunder to rumble on ahead of the wrong who have a right to this night also. Ahead of hooves and beasts we see and the creations of imagery flash-slashed before our eyes.

All of this. All of this – needs to rise and then fall, burn then freeze, undo those locks and throw away all the keys.

Undo them now and open every door. Release those regrets and explore the horizons firing a darkening sky.

"It is beautiful," I said.

And your smile, I remember, refracted and reflected, bisecting that moment in an instant. And you were there, daring me to follow. Holding my hand. Pay nothing for tomorrow, for here the journey ends, and in ending, turns to begin again.

"Take my hand," you said.

The ending has no place here. There is nothing can be done and everything to be undone..

How do we do all this?

Gently – with a kiss and with love.

And then what? As the warm wind rushes to brush my face and your face gazing through me at that sky, that storm, that wish for home and to be one, as any*one* can be.

That and then and that is how it was. No explanations, and all in riddles, of course.

And webs?

The webs are forever and can be seen in some enchanted dreams – like these. Like that. Scattered and random, tattered (some) and abandoned (others).

The webs have neither seam nor stitch into which to pitch those trillion, trillion, trillion souls. No release or tolls. The captured have been captured and the cauldrons stirred for want of a turn of a card. Or a star, troubled and far. Or – by chance – we are overheard a secret wish. Discover this. Your lover's kiss was final, the wine poured, glass raised and a promise made to break this storm, this idle moment that had been destined and preordained. Never questioned. We wax and wane. Wax and wane.

And I see it now. Cold as day. I can feel it now – how it all became this way, not that, disarrayed and confused and lost among all *that*. It makes sense, a reverence to what cannot be believed or agreed to be ever unevered, endeavoured, nevered or evered again.

It all makes sense. Hence to this. Here beneath suns and stars, no cause. Just your eyes looking through mine.

"It is beautiful," I said.

Your eyes said, "*I know.*" Then, "*Take my hand.*"

A las, to understand the clues, we must choose our choices and reveal the guises of our predetermined and every predestiny.

Next to me you lie. Never cried, or said goodbye. There was never *anything* ever to lose. You lie next to me. Your hand is in mine – our horizons assigned. The rhymes are forever rhymed; the love blinding us. Your lines. My lines. Foreveryours. Forevermines. Entangled and twisted. Absolving every question of faith.

And, as our horizons locked and electrics shocked and strobed loaded dice, the thunder tolled and the numbers rolled, rolling every slice of light that might put a pin into something.

But not this day. For this day is our last. Every future, post present and past. Every single solitary authority that decided no more than that.

How could it be?

How could it be? Our final day together. But never expected a web to break.

Oh – dear – God.

For God's sake. We are as we are.

How many storms? How many poems and lines and riddles and rhymes? How many born? Horizons divined. How many mourned? The trillions opening their eyes. Undo the disguise that wrapped them, strapped them into *their* webs. Their beds were left by the dead (remember?). Their heads and skulls were crushed (I do not remember). Or was that just a pay-to-price? Something required by sacrifice? Yet there was never another way to go. There was never a river that flowed so quickly into a stagnant sea. And I see how you and me were undestined to unbegin again.

You saw this.

You unbegun this.

And now the webs are broken.
And now the dead have awoken.
And now the storm has taken what it needs.
And the horses race for what they believe.

D own and down, deeper down we go, lost to the last, the last to know. And so the show turns about to begin. And the edge of the rim sips to a fingertip singing a note of its own. And the world resonates, illuminates and terminates every bone and stone unturned. Because uncovered and undiscovered they rest – whilst storms overhead redress and anoint every new dawn.

Still the cards turn.

Still die and dice are thrown.

Still the numbers roll.

The suites and faces curl for no want of use, played and displayed. There is a truce between the cards and the die. They all work together - same sums, different lives.

The trillions and trillions and trillions each enjoy their share, for beyond here and there are only rumours that true love is party to none of this. And true love (can only be true) if we are to return to our here and now.

Now is for the constant, the note singing from your wine glass, the spurls of a moment, the crest upon which your wish rests. Listen to that note. How that rim sopranos as if ever a second might stop. As if ever a minute might fall from the clock that counts hours and days and forgotten graves as if they were time itself.

Unwind, unrhymed, decipher and undefined. Here we are, caught up in all this. Here every twist and kiss is lost between oracle and historical, future and forever. For ever and ever – *Amen*.

Yet, there we were.
 And here we are.

As if dead to this deadened world. Where souls follow souls, one after the other. Uselessly. Pathetically. Burrowing beneath the earth for cover. Dig in your toes and snuggle down deep. The webs that caused this are only slices of sleep, or death, whichever is preferred.

Yes. Snuggle down deep, my love. As I peek between the veils (fragile and frail) (remember?). Because deep is as deep as a dagger can be drawn. The curtains and nets that separate this are palmed like cards, to deflect all this. The lies and overrides conceal. The circles and squares reveal – few secrets, if any.

Fall we will and crawl we will, into that hole behind that star. It is here we will, like a tempest prevail and blow the entirety of *everything* away.

Deep down, my love.

Close those unclosed eyes.

Sleep, but awake, my love.

See how the rook flies up, up and above, high and alone, gathering, then resting upon his cornerstone.

All that is lost is gathered here once more. Because nothing is lost, ceiling to floor. Nothing even whispered (so quietly you would never know). Evermore and nevermore, evermore alone.

Here we are, my love. In here behind your star, holding hands, unplanned, thrown into the spokes of the infinite, eternal wheel. See how it brakes and in this undoing, makes out as if to be real – yet, clearly, as blurred and broken as broken can be.

You did this.

You broke and separated time.

You chose.

And now everything is underlined.

Everything derailed – line entwined into tangles.

And tangled still as tangled we are, following from afar, we are, *you are*, less than a shard in the click of a broken glass, without ringing, no resonance, no future – perhaps? But continue to circle, bloodied and red. Look at the sky burned garnet. Look! Cuts like a knife. Horses chasing away the last remnants of life.

Those mumbling echoes and sharing of vows and an aisle by which only a promise allows. We cast out those swirls smoothed into plaids and pleats and curls and twirls, befitting the beast. Spires in the sun cast spells of their own and chimes ringing in and ringing on, timed to no time, no tune, no melody, groom, or bride. A symmetry and finality, no less.

Yet we saw the webs forming, even then. Spun into the shadows below them, confettied glades between them. We watched and saw how quickly their small landlords worked, perfect hosts to those that come their way.

Aha! But only a clue. The hint of a scene like the wink of an eye, if you know what I mean. A tip and gipsy warning. The prey are quick to gather, then scatter. I see the confetti caught, pitter-patter, little spider cutting them all loose. Hereafter, beside her as she shakes hair loose and allows whispers into her ear…..so quietly you would never, ever hear?

I pay them no attention, for this day will always be ours, our tower rising churches, your arms full of flowers, it emerges, to colour this mosaic bouquet.

Who is that whispering?

Glistening gold around third finger.

Who are you listening to?

Little voices from the past. Ghosts, almost, scratching messages, casting shadows as shadows cast.

For when we turn alone and the bells and the wells and the wishes and kisses have all gone, we sit up and watch the moon, as we have always done. Count the stars and decide to wait for daybreak – the bride herself.

(the train hurries along)

B ack some way to where and when it really all began. Children playing we were, as I was trying to hold your hand. Was it *really* so long ago? Hidden woods, hidden away, and we played as if lost forever. Climbing trees and scoring hearts and promising never to tell of this. Hearts drawn with branches, romances nobody would understand. White dress. July. Am I.....ever to awaken?

And, as we tumble and play, I say,

"It is beautiful."

And, as I stand and reach you say,

"Then, take my hand."

And we are dancing in and out of the sun, sparkling and skipping as we run, triangled and halved and triangled again. We lie in the grass, voices soft and lamenting when every moment is lost and washed clean and re-readied and reopened and hoping that something might remain – to record all this. In spite of this..... these..... moments.

Fall and we roll. Laugh and hold. Sing out loud and break these slender threads, you would not know they were there. And you are on your back and wide eyed and stack the world behind us. Giggles and wriggles and middles without beginning or end. Head back, hair back, thrown into the shade where cobwebs encroach upon any darkness.

And – as laughter stops, snipped cleanly in half, eyes meet. I thought I saw a whispering there.

Oh – dear – God.

Was I just imagining this?

It *was* beautiful.

(Then, take my hand)

There are no goodbyes or lost farewells. There are no conclusions or illusions, no disturbed intrusions that might set a spark to the twilight, set the bride and groom running home.

As the sun sets behind us, contrasts us against our dimming sky, we still run and hide and disguise and surprise and throw innocence at the night. For we have not, as yet, begun to even yet count the nearest star.

Nightmares graze in the haze of distant fields. They await the groom and evening's return. They await to run free, as only they and you and I can see. And we await also.

Tonight I count the stars and I count them short. It maybe I have forgotten, each one caught onto a loop its own. I count again, know them all, every single flicker and their place and where they belong.

Is it just my imagining – or do I wrong every right to be tightened and turned?

Tighten the thread the snuffed and the dead, splice the strands hint-tinted instead of the finest shreds unpicked and split, lit by those faraway stars.

I can no longer count. Every thread is a soul, journeyed devout, inside and without. Every spell is a spirit conjoured and doubted, for mystical and wistful we play our little cards, extraordinary and bizarre, we could deal ourselves so short.

Nothing is nothing, no matter how it is made out.

Instead…..I look for a sign that might define exactly and precisely how it is all meant to be. And if someone, if somebody were able to break destiny. How, of all this, we should realise we are already free? Or what of this lie? That cannot decide. Do ghosts slide between worlds and whisper whilst they cross? Is it they who are free? Or, perhaps, it is *they* who are not. Guardian angels unable to untether their knots.

Oh, ridiculous sublime! Such tedium in these where-with-alls regarding time.

So where are the lines? The holes and circles? The earthfulls of emptied graves? So where are we now? Lost count of the stars. The hellos and hoorahs, the cellos and charades and equidistant farewells.

The hells and heavens and houses awake. Every layer and level, every angel and devil, every soul freed from the chains unstraightened – all for a second of freedom.

Because – This was not meant to be.

Because – This was *not* meant to be.

You and me. Upon a train. Through a storm. Not yet readied to be turned or buried, or removed from those webs.

Not yet!

There had been no time.

The wine of the groom had bloomed behind him as he had waited for the dawn and bride's arrival. Neither rivals nor lovers, no sunrise that smothered or burned out her bridal wake.

Not meant to be.

You and me.

Like this.

Not.

Definitely. Not meant to be

Help me raise myself and clear my vision. Help me raise my head that I might watch the skies unfold.

All ruddied against agitated skies. For that is an act of twilight – as it is also an act of sunrise.

Unable to decide.

We should be riding those horses.

As horizons divide.

Cannot decide.

Who is alive – or who is dead.

A ye! We played before a storm. Our very first one. Rumbles and rattles and overhead battles crackling and chattering, light spattering against an x-ray red. Such laughter amid all this. Just children in the heavy rain, booming lanes, drains sucking back the essence of this, this first moment, first kiss.

We laugh all the more, as the booms bare deeper, juddering into the core of the earth, immersed into foreverness, curved when togetherness had not guessed two children like this. That a kiss could seal the heavens, rolling and trembling and assembling turrets against the hiss of intense rain. And a kiss that became the last, the first, the one and the same.

But had our cards been dealt too quickly, too swiftly for lines to align and a web designed to hold us? Or enfold us and wrap us and trap us to a purpose unbeknown to ourselves?

Unexpected card. Unexpected turn. Unexpected indeed.

Connected from then to the taste of our lips; omitted to ponder upon this – simplicity.

Here is that moment to frame.

Soaked to the skin.

We had danced in the sun.

Climbed trees and turned when the sky became grey.

Yet we stayed.

And welcomed the rains.

Then the umber that became our first storm.

Convinced of our innocence she plays forlorn, thunderous and shocking; unlocking our wheel that we might run and kneel before the grace of God.

Maybe not He.

Maybe, even, not at all.

But what *something* was not running as the thunder tolled and the lightening severed the moonrise and the rain lashed and whipped the wind into our eyes? A creator stood upon his theatre and bellowed and laughed as fate had slipped a card.

This – so difficult to reveal.

So undoing to explain.

Perhaps, enough to say for as much as I have spoken, each and every line was broken.

However, lines repair and most, if not all, prepare the webs and pulled them tight that they might run simple and straight, such lines when made are quick and unassuming.

Okay.

Okay.

Okay.

If I may touch and attempt to make sense of all this.

This kiss was truly no more than a togethering of lips. No more than this. But, yes, it cast a spell beyond the veil whilst linemakers were distracted.

Does that make sense?

Not even yet?

Okay.

The temptation is to lie here and allow everything to recede. Such a temptation. To leave it, no reason to believe this, no reason to pray – unless you feel a need.

Last try – to move from the then up to now.

Children.

Storm.

Kiss.

Such a seed to sow.

God knows.

We roll and laugh and run, soaked and elegantly, beautifully one. Even then.

The look in your eyes.

As I see into mine.

Gorgeous and sweetness and devilness combined.

Jeered by the thunder.

Prompted by that storm.

Is that what was happening?

Before we ran home.

Is that, or what, or who, or not?

That pulled our lips together and loosened the knots, even from way back then?

Difficult to explain.

But I am trying.

And as the rains chased us from woodland toward home and we giggled and spun our heads full of quarrelsome red, red skies.

A gain, the heat returns. A thousand suns – or so it seems – each combined into one, and pursuing the path it has always done.

Like needles into crevices and stone, no concern, just a blurring that cannot decide.

But, where was I?

Answering with questions, of course. Because it is questions that reveal the most.

How should the bride dance under the bloom of forevered twilights? How such delay?

Now. This returned sun, comes like a fire from the dawn, explodes as the morning burns away and the heat of the day infuses and seeps, excuses and leaves, and loses as waves upon waves upon waves return, rise and fall and scroll away.

I am aware of here. The *hereness*, wherever it is. I am aware of your nearness, whatever or however we seemed to miss this. This here and now as the sun turns around and pushes and radiates and reheats the world. For I have been pulled into this hole behind a star. We have fallen into this teeming bazzar. I am here, but – dearest God – alone.

The valley of the shadow of something or other. Some shadow from which we are yet to recover. As lovers embrace and promise and dance, so our horizons pull a card and chance an entrance to open a door. Allow a way from here to forever, from here to whenever, if only that card would turn.

But destiny's languid, yet specific race has another face. These twists and turns of riddled embrace, spaced between measures to a faraway place.

I am counting now.

My first is this spirit, the second your soul, third is an angel, inconsoled. Fourth and fifth a wish upon a star – they are tricks, because all of this is a rune and a rhyme. Bringing you near, but never to the line, or the circle, or the star, thine and mine. Or to the edge after you had said,

"Take my hand."

Because there was another storm coming. It could be seen in the sky. You and I. Me and you.

Soft dew upon the webs.

Where the dust of the dead had come to their rest.

Where undiscovered bones, blessed and forgotten, festered and rotten, powder the invisible lines, threads and empty beds.

And *still* this all continues, when, sincerely, I have made the decision to stop. Carries on despite closure. Despite the storm, the empty lantern swinging in a darkly hall. This is all it could ever have been. An attempt to reveal whatever it is that brought us here.

So lay back and rest and I will rest beside you.

Tilt your head back into the whispers that stack the world behind us. And I will lay my head next to yours; wrap my hand in yours. Breathe my breath into your emptiness. Snuggled together. Watching the glow of a lowering sky. This is why words will not stop, nor wine induced rhyme drop one split second from our stopped clock.

Oh – dear – God.

Just remember.

The red horses in our final sky.

Just remember.

It was you – not I – that chose to die.

I merely followed.

And now all too late as the universe disintegrates and crumbles and tumbles to nothing. Fine dust, I have noticed, tick-tocking, clogging all the clocks, locking all the locks, dust of the dead, forcing time to stop.

The finest and smallest the largest has become. Has grown into an army of one. Mighty and enormous, blown up from the pit.

This is it.

This is where I lie. Counting the stars and fireflies.

This is where we lay.

And this is where we end.

Come on!

Send an angel if you are unable to meet. The dust and heat defy me. They choke and scold, as if melancholy were drawing breath back into our undergrowth and snagged beds. Where we rest our heads.

I shall await. But make it quick. Hesitation destroys even that army of dust.

Where are you?

I am unable to follow.

I am unable to join in this defiance.

Are the gods so angry? Our alliance – Love.

Love.

Love.

Love.

And the chain has been split. The lines have been turned, twisted and slit with the blade of the surreal. Congealed blood blunted. Hooded and cowled and hunted – feel the knife edge slicing every second into a world each its own. Feel the derangement of it all. The insanity which we call the Now.

Oh – dear – God.

Is this it?

Is this Your light?

The empty lantern still swings in a darkening hall.

The cloak and the shawl raised to hide – something.

What could it be?

Would you whisper it to me?

Would you mime the clue that I may read your lips – the same lips I kissed so innocent.

Can that *something* be named?

Contained?

Even though I am unable to follow such hollowed hearts.

So dispel the spell that spools each to a way out of here. Foretell the rolling bell that has fallen – calling and tolling as it turns and the hammer strikes and the broken rhythm demands decision to pull all together again.

Fortune crosses her fingers, just as we had crossed our hearts. Crosses and chains engrained with the dust as we embark and depart. And the dead mark this as a new beginning – and those who are not, less forgiving, for they know not, and knots in deed are only lines turned and returned to lock such fickle destinies.

But, yes, we embark upon this journey of sorts; this destination to an unnamed station, imaginary ship between ports, crossing the vale as if we might set sail into that hazed sky, nailed to the boards, pointed toward – this place of absent ghosts.

The dead have risen and the graves lie empty, their dust billowed up, spinning through these ill-defined illusions, infused into their own delirium. The puppet theatre chatters, wondering at the strings scattered about them, freed, but unable to move. Every marionette, twisted and contorted, broken by the hooves of chance, yet unable to dance, the entrance to this liberation of life beyond death – and those horses racing ahead of the storm.

Distorted distortions and motions where these are applied. For there is no time to decide. Remember, the clocks are sticking as the dead return. Remember the locks are jammed and the weathervanes turned against the wind. Remember the undoing of it all? How you had *seen* the moment in a moment within a moment so small? A particle in a universe rolled into layers and lines and elaborate designs and webs that maze away forever.

An exit through a door.

Nothing more.

A look in your eyes – decide.

That is what you saw.

Reflected in the window as our carriage hurried on.

Watching the skies of a developing storm.

As the horses run, cloudy and red and ahead of the breakers, as if against rocks on a razored shore. Crashing and whooming, furiously booming and colliding with all that it may.

But the day – remember – we played. Children in a storm and a kiss had begun as a snag in this zig-zagged web of ours.

Oh, so sweet.

And beautiful, too.

Allowed you to see it all so clearly. So real and defined. Just as the clocks were about to chime. Just as time prepared to move a second on. And the mechanism seized. And the cogs of evermore freeze and lock and stop and keys no longer turn. We turn, and turn against the waves that raise mountains before the rocks that stand their ground and slowly erase. We turn and turn and return. We rise and fall, sink and roll with the errant currents that busily winde, blindingly mis-signed, allowing us to nowhere.

In that reflection in a carriage window. That is where the undoing began. That is where you held my hand and took me beyond that door to here. That is where toward a fold unfolded, you blessed the unblessed and pulled us into this curtain call. Afterall, the blushing sky had played its role and the horses of perchance were chased by even darker souls.

This is where we are, then. Or, at the very least, behind a star and hidden in a hole. Bizzare, then, we should be held here, as control is readdressed and the guests that we are, allowed to pick at the threads, whilst the beds of the dead are abandoned and the graves we thought full are vacuums, black rooms, lightless, oblong and cold.

Threads split, frayed, tripped and played within the loom. Slackened and tightened, vibrato enlightened as the rhythms and rhymes combine unknown to the metronome *click*, and the metronome *tock*, for this is where it stopped – inbetween beats.

And as our lines meet.

And the stars blur.

And the moon glooms behind the clouds.

Yet lucid when a break allows.

And our hands touch.

As the world rushes on past.

And our anchors are lifted as we drift and surface and serve us free, encouraging us to believe.

The night settles in now. I can feel the cold in my bones as I lie here in this pool of unconsciousness. Quickening around me, gathering in, like that monstrous beast we call fate. Too little, too late. Now *you* wait there as I die here. What never-end-ment were you expecting?

And as the moon wheels around and the earth is unwound and floated, coil spring loose for rewind. This is where we find and draw that line between the real and the vague. This is where we break upon the shore. The difference that you saw reflected in that window.

See you. See me. How could this ever be called destiny? I see you seeing me, in your eyes a madness (almost), as you smile and I smile back, and once again encounter the sky and the vanishing stars we have counted as ours. Of the changing that bled scarlet into storm; a blackness we call home. Where kisses seal against the next deal fortune plays us, yet waves us merrily on.

All I can do is remember. All I can do here is be here and play your puzzles, though I struggle against the cold. As I drop into an icy embrace, this place of here and now.

Oh, dear God.

Where are we now? Can you not hear me calling as I sink into this pit? Can you not hear my heart break as I reach to have you near? Come! Steer me as a ship, as a wave raised a mountain against the shore. Come! Guide me, that I may finally slide sweetly, explore each kiss as the rook soars, collecting his leaves and bones. Such aloneness upon his isolated dream, stones stacked onto this gathering.

Where are you now? Do not desert me here within this cage-cum-pit-cum-hole-behind-a-star. Wherever you are, you cannot be *that* far away. There is not a star we have not counted, nor a moon we have not wanted, nor a storm from which we would ever run. This was your turn to twist and break the seal. Everything that had seemed real. Break and deal an unknown hand; a card as yet unplayed. There are no delays tracing all those hallowed hearts. What would you do? And where would you be? If it was me I would hide behind the hidden. I would ride beyond the driven skies, spliced and ribboned, forbidden for the likes of love.

Yet above us the rook, unhooked from any tethers, black feathers, tattered, oiled as a robe. See how he soars through the storms that have caused us to do this – finally – sweep away all that you see, smash and destroy this endless expediency; this rush befitting a whole that is splitting, to a moon that is drifting, sifting the dust of the dead. Could never be said their voices would crumble unheard. It is here we amass and recover the last, first to the last, every single of every trillioned soul. Pulled together, drawn forever, to whenever a moment unfolded.

This is it. This is where we are. Crossed between a hole and a missing star. The charades of life are enough, suffice, to enable or disable karma. We linger and honour this ridiculous collusion of delusions and insipient confusions designed to elude. We await, with a full heart, the promises of emptiness given to fill our cups.

In all this silence and nothingness it is as if I see some purity. I try to untangle, but doing so tangle all the more. My opening and unweaving have no revelation I can think of. I remember; but only occasional scenes. I forget more than as yet I expect. But I do know this. The spirit of my love. The constant upon which we are woven and chosen to be here. Wait upon the periphery, just beyond the circle of complicity where we call this world our throne and manage to stumble home here among the bones of defaulted dust.

So be it. Time to move on.

Still the cold is drawn into me and through me for here, wherever I lie, it enters and centres, frigid as a winter sky. Sparkles starlight frozen sigh – a puff of frost in a breath, a ruffle of the little time we have left.

My soul is empty. My lips unkissed. My arms no longer around you. Your heart not beating that beat. I lower before you, but cannot see you. Not to be left here. Let me gather you up. Enough is enough. Let us free ourselves from all of this that you have done. You have done!

Oh, dear God.

C larify.
    Clarify.

The tide has turned.

Returned. ——

Spoken clearly.

Listen.

Pure as the sounding bell.

Empty your heart and you will hear the ringing and chiming and rhyming of every *now*. Because every *now* is an estranged rearranged reality.

Here is the reality.

A train pulls in and pulls upon our hearts.

We are wedded as one as this train departs.

Remembering our stops and starts and nameless destinations. Our tickets and flickers of other stations, flashing past as this and that, unknown, unheard, platforms between here and there.

The glare from the wine as our glasses entwine and the world beyond our windows rush by.

The intoxicating bouquet as we whisper our wishes. And we raise our glasses, soft kisses, because we have arrived. Yet, strangely, the skies have clouded and horses are riding the range. Shrouded as purples engage, see them racing away.

"It is beautiful," I say.

"Then take my hand."

I see you in a reflection as eyes decide to a moment pause and change; deranged, "Nothing will ever be the same after this."

A second, split-second, without a cause.

And I followed you to the door.

Storm – exactly as our first – hammering stones, powdering the skeletons and broken bones, white washed and bleached, adrift and lifted and left upon some faraway beach. Kiss, temporary goodbye and farewell.

'Goodbye!'

Farewell!

My love.

I kind of remember the fall. The pull. The rolling vortex of it all. The hand-in-hand, never-let-go, sucked into oblivion, trillioned and trillioned and trillioned. I remember the ghosts that rushed past, like clashed cymbols, too loud for whispers, dispersed and scattered. Bring it back. Sucked back and heaping the world behind us.

Where were the words as we spun?

Words inbetween me and you?

"I love you!"

"I love you!"

And then the world was gone.

The cold burns in, poured upon my beginnings and my never endings. Descending those spiral stairs that climb and descend, world without end – *Amen*.

Amen. Amen And Amen.
There is no end.

There is no beginning, middle or angel to guide you. There is no god who can hide you away and make a secret turning. For there is a price upon your head, the total z-read when you are finally dead, but not a hint instead of the debt for which you are incurring.

White-washed away.

Bleached and lighteninged.

You must not frighten yourself over so many idle nightmares. Climb or descend those stairs. Choice is yours.

Close all the doors.

Look up and about you.

Look down and around you.

Take the handrail and make a choice.

There is no voice to follow.

No song to be sung or head hollowed for a hallow's eve.

Dark as that.

No tune, or rhyme, or constellation.

No zodiac.

Or spiritual destination.

Take the rail and make a choice.

Up or down.

About and around.

The mouse left click as the right click clock aftershocks run on to a halt. And you are left there standing as the bolts are shunted into their holes and locked and stopped and tolls priced for payment.

Coins at the ready if you feel you must cross. Delayed too long at the stairwell if you could not have made a decision. The condition is your soul. The coins are merely rolled along the board of chance, or spun roulette to see if you would advance against the odds.

Anyway.

Blue is grey.

And red meets black.

And sunsets narrow through the slats of peeped reflections. The conception that we would ascend above this folly.

It does not matter anymore.

I wager my breath.

And raise with a heartbeat.

It is all over now.

Does not matter anymore.

It is all over now.

The waves slacken against the shore.

The ships flounder.

The rook soars into a lazy eve.

As the night steals in.

And the flight of those who thought they would win.

Fall heads into pillows.

Troubled sleep.

Within a dream of slumbering stars.

If these were all ours we would count them all over again. Split the hemispheres, splice the perimeters and reclaim each weathervane as ours. The pointer turns back against the winds of creation as each and every explanation overturns and overruns the dividing lines.

Destiny derailed, ships unsailed, sunk and sank and banked beneath broken harbours. Journeys magnificently annulled below the storms at the end of this world.

There is a sleepy silence at the beginning of a new world, an eye opening slow-motioning, ocean of awakening. A softness radiates and fills the soft graves, illuminates even the lowest glow, because there is no darkness here. Only light, as soft as a kiss between veils, as pure as crystal-trailed stretches before sunrise, pulled straight and likewise serenaded as a song to flood early morning.

And, slowly, we too, as spirits might alight free to unhook and untie the ever within the finite. This yours and mine might recover or uncover some other *now*ness, something that surrounds us and beckons to follow.

This blessed *now* allows a wistful wish, a mistiness between shifted veils; a twisty turning where we follow ourselves running backwards. To where beginnings began?

A flowered glade spangling bloom and blossom. A serenade fades whilst a melody shifts across them, tipping as bees squeeze into the pursed lips, with dust from the sun. For ever we have come, buzzed and running, man and woman – but, infact, just boy and girl.

A tidal colour criss-crossed as breezes discover each other through these openings between trees. A fountain of greens, serenely, dreamily sprayed, spluttered and dazed. A massing together of feathered and flashed, skipped and enveloping our energy. And as these energies combine and we walk in line as lines of narrow paths steer ways of their own, and we walk alone, one behind the other, there is a quickening of the heart, a crazy, yet delicious, thought.

We are innocently arrived. Innocence our guide. Had followed a stream that ran into the trees and then out again. Following it along as if we belonged here forever. Up, beyond a gate, and over and under a hedge where edges and ledges break beneath our feet, and further ahead to meet fields and distant woods. And as the stream runs away on a way of its own, away to some unreachable home we have never been, or seen, or ever likely to have even dreamed of ever dreaming. Here we are seeing and belonging. Here we are wishing and longing for nothing more than we have here. Here we are – unfolding between one another. Here we are – illusive, uncovering these delights of ensuing nights. But – not too soon – as our imagined world defaults to the loom of where we should be, and where we should also belong.

I save the moment as I would a butterfly in a jar, or a firefly – same jar – different star, different world from where we are hiding.

Sliding down a bank we were, toward the wood we had marked between gated and abated along the way. Nevertheless, we rise, heads above this brilliance, chasing the skies – or were the skies chasing us?

July firing on all cylinders, impermeable heat as her pistons strike and the strokes match strokes, powering the afternoon on. Her haze shimmering a harem dance, advances each second on. Perspiration trickling down her neck, hair pulled around, nape soft and slightly wet, revealing that delicious thought sensation caught behind my eyes, filed and stored pending authorisation.

At some point below a tree. You have drawn circles, but I am not sure. Say they are hearts for those far apart and longing to be near. A shrug will suffice as I watch your face and you draw another with a stick along the soil and intermittent grasses (sparse in the coil of shadowed shade).

"*This one is a circle*," as the stick is guided around. "*Somewhere to hide in. Until you are found.*"

"Ha! Ha!" as I step into your circle.

"*Now are protected and cannot be seen.*" Then, "*Here!*" and you follow me in.

"*We are invisible.*"

Your body is close to mine. Perspiration runs. Smoothly down. Can smell your hair. Face infront of mine. Lips drawn into a little smile.

"Invisible?"

"*Yes. As long as we remain in our circle of spells.*"

"Invisible?"

"*Because this is our enchantment.*"

Can smell your breath. Taste your voice. "It is a tree branch!"

"*Not any old tree! It's a supernatural tree.*"

"Of course," I say nervously, impervious to reality, purposed to finality, hovering between the two. Touch her lips with mine.

"*Oh!*" and stand back.

I do not move. Can feel the magic. "Invisible, did you say?"

"*Was that a kiss?*"

"I do not know what it was."

"*I think it was trying to be a kiss.*"

"You said we were invisible?"

"*Yes, we were.*"

And our lips meet again, gentle – but, this time, out of the circle uninvisibled, for all to see.

Then stop!

Move away.

And the circle has gone as we climb astride and along an oak, old and twisted, poking its branches into the eye of the surreal – keeping us hid, mid-afternoon, not knowing why or how or what to come.

Such sorcery!

"We are on a ship," I say, "Can't you see?"

"*I do see.*"

"About to set sail to a faraway land. Just you and me."

"*I do see. I shall cloak our ship in magic, too. Just me and you.*"

And so it should be; upon an ocean and then a

sea, sails set high and filled, flapping and billowed, unfollowed to our horizon beyond.

Allow the day to run its course. Allow the ships and horizons to return to their source. Allow the circles and hearts, the fits and starts and unreadable parts of an unread book. Look! Are we not here again? Look! Same as it was. Watch, because – here comes the storm to discover. One at a time, procession in line, designed to follow one another. Designed to even the score. But you laugh all the more. And I laugh with you and we run together as it gathers and draws in behind us.

"Invisible indeed!"

Now.
It is a dream within a dream; a sleep within the unconscious. Only to awake, eyes closed, lids locked, soul blocked, stocks and chains (almost), prostrated and broken – but not dead. Aware you are there – you are here and so very near. Bloodied sky. Dead and abandoned.

Rooftop grey, mad-hattered parades – the ghosts of nevermore stranded. Jeckle and Hyde hidden, forbidden visions. A condition unwound where this merry-go-round uncoils and loosens all those threads. Allows in the other darkness. That which weds one-eye-opened to death, one-eye-closed to the breath that blows it all away. Unioned into nothingness. Promised to the everness of unbeing.

Closer and closer. Cross-stitched into a silent scream. The colossus has risen and crystallised to shatter as bones to dust, to clog the cogs of stained pipe-dreams. Puffs of such, not worth so much as a jot, for all that might have been. Lost among all that emptiness as it peels away, diseased and unbelieved.

Closer still, this will in deed speed the slowest to their graves, lure the abandoned and the strays, devour the lost criss-crossed, powdered rocks and routes and roads and those who fell before the storm.

Close as a breath. Close as a sigh. Drawn into this lie of so-called fortune. Close as a vein pulsing way in and way out of this distortion.

Closer and closer and closer yet. Listen to that breath, that sigh that sets before it shatters. Everything that ever mattered. Everyone that scattered dust into this dream. Stopped it clean. Broken motion, stopped and frozen, ground to a grated halt.

All within a second – and only a fraction of that, exact past and present, exactly that. *That* which pulls the web apart. *That* between the beats of a heart, between two moments – *inside* that pause inbetween.

We saw all of this – our eyes wide open. And the darkness that slept unawoken and in an instant released from its own carousel within the constant. Now it scrambles at the announcement that every path coincides and hastily, roughly retied – to whence or where or ever or never. Continuity has been broken. The beast has now awoken – to repair as best can. His tools are lies and deception. His ploys a bevelled reflection backing back against the mirror of reverse.

We lie here.

We touch.

But not.

We wait here.

Together.

But for what?

We can sense the spirit arising. Pervading. Dissecting. Fractionallising. Checking the new knots in every thread. Checking they are aligned and not crossed with the dead or unawoken.

We lie here.

We *are*.

Somewhere in this tangle.

We remain here.

Innate.

But *our* thread has been broken – dangling – loose.

If he will bite. If he can be hurried to the repair. Such a lair! Ha! I feel he is already on the run.

That if one loop should break – all being held together as one – one single loop (should I say thread) (no matter how strong), the whole implodes and the fabric blows out and in upon itself.

You did that.

We did that.

Here he comes! To fix his broken web. Can you feel the twitching as he arrives? All his destinies? All his disjointed lies? All his sleepy unconscious-awoken twists and turns, his feasts and undiscovered bones?

Senses we are here, but cannot see us. Fixes and

splices with expedience entices us his knot to hold as he pulls each part together. Pay no heed, my love, his deed is done and there is no clue where this loop of thread will run.

Are we as one as yet?

Have I been found?

The beast has ears opened.

Listening for your sound as he tightens that thread tight and around many fingers – waiting for a sigh.

Then, come find me in my dreams. Allow me – despite this state – unconscious, but awake. Close my eyes, though they are closed. Fall away, though I am frozen in my fall. Despite this. Despite that. Despite everything. Despite it all.

The sun rises again. Skewers heat into rocks into dust, into the atoms and the space that divides them into fractions, rooted, mooted, square-rooted and squared again. The sun – fission collissioned particles, deflected empty and void, reflected and confuses yet embroiders each separate star, every minute shard, expanding at the speed of light, as infinity collapses and the rook rises into full flight.

Down and down and deeper down. Further and farther, deeper and darker. Into and inward, spinning surrendered, hopelessly drawn, gravitational forms that align time and untime.

Then, untimed and underlined, the rook gains lift, soars and swirls up above all this. Above the gathering of forevers, cornered and lost, black feathers twisted to a cross – whispers of the uncertainty below.

Skim the empty doorways cluttered with symbols and runes, over the abandoned tombs, the wounds cut into rock. The grooms and brides, left to die, below these contortions.

The world waits.

Waits.

And waits.

The clock has stuck.

Only the rook takes his time, travelling straight lined beyond the cornerstones. Chequered and squared, broken and repaired, cracked and broken. The plates of the earth are the custodians of our deeds. Moving if there is a need. Or holding as forces are applied and mountains rise and oceans sink and the twilights fall away.

Here, the purple upon which the circle completes in incandescence, essence to meet and deplete, sweeps across the silence. Science and lore engage, just as evening and night fade unto the morning. Just as skies and storms reform without warning.

Still the rook is aloft, flying as high as he may, as high and as far without becoming lost. His rise and collection of scattered possessions, his gathered towers of unremembered hours and broken things beneath the beat of wings, merely collections and obsolete directions. Yet here they are – piled as high and as far as could be seen: every little movement, second, anything that has ever been and then discarded.

And the higher he climbs the further and farther behind unwinds and every distance resigns to having lost the cause. Lost the source. Lost the fragment of everness that became neverness. Lost, but collected (because *everything* is collected). Lost, but misplaced here – somewhere – among the towers of stacked happenings, words, thoughts and dreams.

Keep searching.

Chase those far horizons.

Rise upon the thermals that lift you up and on.

Glide tower to tower, (searching) for something that you forgot. Something forgotten? No! You know exactly for what you are (seeking). It is there. Somewhere. (remember – nothing is ever lost).

D o I sleep yet?
  Still awake.

But – yes –asleep.

Oh – dear – God.

We ran beneath a storm.

Fused beneath a storm.

Beginning and ending, both born from the One..

Dressed in white – always.

Listening to ghosts and watching the skies. Awaiting the horses you knew would rise. Messengers – say the voices, and the choices you have to make there. Watch – that you may see what they say. Listen – this vision is coming. An awakening. The dead lie waiting. The crushed and broken, the lost and undiscovered, enemies and lovers, all gathering at the gates. The dust reforming as they wait. The clouds darkening and filling, heavy and laden, forbearers of doom, awaiting the groom.

Wait until the sky glows red.

As red as wine. As you are mine. Let us share our oneness, our lines and webs. What was it you said, about the ghosts? Strange hosts they are. That bring us this far. What was it you said about fixed destinies? I was barely listening. Come next to me. Let us share this wine together. As our train hurries on. Bride and groom. Honeymoon. Draw your circles that we may climb into the unseen. Dig out the hole behind a star that we may hide from these crazy dreams. Draw a line, that we may step over it. But, I think, we are already over and beyond that line, passed beyond the star, encircled, butterflies in a jar, fireflies, that's what we are. Watched. Awaited. Primed and baited. The line has been thrown. The trillions and trillions and trillions – they all wait alone, but together. This is their chance, their moment, to capture forever.

But our train hastens on, past stations and junctions, platforms and place, names and landmarks, quickening our pace. Engine swiftening as if quickening this continuity to the final thread of inevitability. As if headlong rushed to smash this stability, break it forever, crush and destroy this pretence of ever and ever – *again*.

Softly the fall away dissolves without a thought. It distils, unfilled and empty. It loosens itself from the slackening crawl. It frees itself from the syrup and slime we tag time. It dislocates and isolates, calibrates itself against the nothing that was. Dreams wander in. Strange guests on the rim of reality that could never be. They mingle and mime to all that nonsense signed to make some kind of sense. They nod and agree – all this ridiculous continuity has no meaning at all if we are, indeed, really unable to do anything whatsoever.

So, if we ever were able to turn a table, or disable this preposterous notion of time. If ever we were here or there, or there or here, or anywhere near or faraway, this line, then, has already been crossed.

Is this sliding a sliding into sleep?

Random zeros.

Zeros add zeros add zeros.

I am already pleasantly adrift, spiralled and kissed, by a tree among trees, within a wood amid these. You are dressed in black. Negative earth. We have reversed. The rook towers stacked around us. Seeking and searching, pulling them apart. Somewhere among these, somewhere around or within these, is that moment that brought us here. Somewhere, despite all these oddments and twisted, broken collections is that thought, word, or instruction that left us and held us abandoned.

Where are we searching?

To who or what person?

To what in fact are we seeking?

Can it be held aloft?

Like a trophy?

How do you hold a moment?

(If you can find it)

Amid all *this*!

And what would we do with it, if it could ever be found?

Nothing.

Zero plus zero plus zero.

Absolutely.

Nothing.

Then, why do we seek that which cannot be found?

"I am searching for you."

I see you. I do. Never seen you in black. What does it mean? Look at you. Like that. You're smiling, but never arriving. Our destination is somewhere too far away. Our constellations entwine, for a time, and zodiacs distract the never from the now. And the elements and cloaks and veils and shrouds as deep earth and dampness allow – we dig fingernails into this bitter flesh. Dark eyed divine, we *are* entwined.

Never the never. Never ever. Never would darkness bow so low. Never – not ever, could blackness pull to-and-fro, up from the depths from so very far below. Never in this world, or universe, or cosmic lee was there ever, could there ever be another you and me, me and you.

And you are so beautiful.

"Come, take my hand."

"No! Let us wait together. A little longer – because I will lose you. Because you're running away.

"Not from you!"

"No."

"I will always be with you."

"Always?"

"Here. Let me draw a circle. I will point you to a star. Follow my finger, see? Can you see that far?"

"It is one of ours."

"I will meet you there. In a hole behind. Where nobody can see. Do you love me?"

"With all of my heart."

"Do you forgive me?

"Always."

Smiles beguile and envelope me. Your eyes and clarity develop these crisp, pencilled margins. Your breath runs beside me, sweetly, completely, overwhelming me.

"Behind that star?" you say.

"I will be there."

And now you are not with me and I am searching through these towers still. The rook flies high above the hill of a zillion tombs as the wombs have been emptied and lost and the waiting have found, to their cost, that such freedom means nothing at all.

L ace-winged and scant, seasons advance. The autumns and summers, the winters and springs, darkness into light, as each to the other clings for its own survival. Webbed and shadowed, good and bad roads all lead to the same semaphored arrival.

The dream has stalled! Now and here and where with all I stand, looking out at a star, secretly bizarre, a hole whereby to hide in, until we meet again.

Sweet love.

Dressed in black.

That is what you have done.

So.

And how to end all of this?

Draw it all to a close?

How – indeed – to disassemble all this, and put it back before it froze and glazed and broke into layers? How – indeed – to return to a time when unfreed we followed our lines? Despite this, our each-otherness combined and love was definite and true.

So, where are you, my love?

What a cost!

Through crystals and spheres and various years and broken and unspoken overtures we paraded and serenaded and emptied our hearts. Through relinquished kiss-and-tells and abandoned farewells and misguided spells we cast one upon another. Through broken dreams and lucid denes and dales and sleepy vales eroded and groved, deep as valleys go, deeper than we know, along weathered walls, sandstoned, trees tall, we flow like a flooded river; rushing and pushing on. There is a song we play against the rocks, mossed and massed, found and lost, over and under, beneath the hills, pure and clear and sparkling. There is a momentum that pushes on, a continuum that spreads out into every overflow, floods wrecklessly into everything we know, overspills and kills and drowns all those who reap but never sow. There is a shower gentle, soaks the mantle draped over dry ground. But we spin in and spin around, entering and exiting before we are found. We gush and rush and quickly hurry on. We are not here long enough to belong.

Splendid and amended we resume our idle play. Keepsakes and deep lakes we submerge and re-enter here. Through tunnel and spring and channels twisting as we turn, we run, as one. Through chasm and cave, over unmarked grave, our saviour and saved, over lost and depraved, we submerge, emerge, but never evade.

Castling rook to king, we are the energy paralleling the home frontier. Back to back. The attack is as if contracted/exacted – death to all against us.

But swords raised and armoured armies gaze out toward their charge. Blood beating, hearts racing, they clasp steel whilst facing the very end.

We flow effortlessly on, up, over ribbling, rabbling waters that have wound here once again, despite the tight corners and turns and auroras and halos and dayglows, on and on.

We slip unnoticed, closest to the wavering edge, brushing, flushing out the beds within which every home was made. We siphon and steal, we take as we wheel our way onward, down toward the sea. We crash over rocks and blast and smash against the locks that would pretend to hold us here. We rise, surprised and wide-eyed open. We gather and surge, purge the very cell that would keep us here. Feel the rush, the hush and pause as we tinkle and jingle then simply roar and cascade down valleys laid into rock, fashioned into stone. It is this we have become. It is this that makes us one. On and on. Deeper to go. Help me! This flow is beyond my control. Rushing. Rushing on.

A nd I am here. Fluid and nearly near, nearly risen, nearly cleared; but not in the sight of God. I am here, raising my eyes to a land that lies unforgiven.

Where am I now?

You dip and dart and somehow evade, fading before I find you, tumbling – a waterfall and torrent, a sweeping intolerance that escapes between the straights of a moment.

Where are you now?

Why! Right here, of course.

Straddling wild, red horses.

Pulling upon their manes.

Kicking in and kicking out.

Lost within and lost without.

Your star awaits you.

Why do you doubt?

Stop running away – turn about. Turn and turn. For, as yin meets yang you are lost, no doubt. The everything interlocks. The unbelievers, the deceivers, the givers and devout. Turn and turn and turn again. Face forward, pledge our vow. Nothing behind or before – there is only the *now*.

Here is yin.

Here is yang.

One is one, the other none.

One is love (gone but never gone).

One is one.

Two add into none.

Cancelled and wholed.

Voided and initialled.

Logged and locked.

The fuse wire fizzles.

Locked and logged.

The initials are His.
Beast and He similar or same.
And so the game continues.
And so, here within you and without.
Cast those doubts aside.

Ride the river as the rook delivers another trinket to another tower. Ride the horses, these forces belong to another power.

The time has come.
    The time has gone.
Time and no-time.
The two are one.
Time has come.
Your web awaits you.
Time has gone.

Lost and misplaced you are torn and twisted away. You are played, we are greyed out of this developing blackness, its exactness is in fact less than a moment on, cut and precise, into the slenderest slice of Om.

Black rook, red horses, chariots and a train, a storm gathering, melting one into the same. The refrain of thunder and score pulling at the reins, splaying the feathers and hammering on the floors. Seek and you shall find, running from where we are – a strange way to find a star. Somebody closed all the doors.

If I can but see it, I can point and spirit follow. Somewhere to rest inside that hollow. And, perhaps, on looking down, make a sense – if sense is allowed.

Seek and you shall find.
Push and the door shall open.
And the windows and attics.
And the gates and paddocks.
Revealed – a line toward that star.
Point, then.
(do we flutter in our jar?)
As the horses are freed.

And you are able to see from where you are, world as it overflows and lowers, as it overloads and lures, as it follows its own contours back into the web.

See how it screens out the clarity. How it double-folds and fogs and rolls – hocus-pocus and out of focus. The trillion, trillion, trillion souls queue waiting.

See *that* which stirs the cauldron ties the knots of this world, whispers into the ears of white dress girls, laughs and steers them away from the turning motion – full of secrets and potions and notions of undoing what should not be undone. Allow them to grow, but never letting go. Whispers and whispers. Is that how these sisters of yours are beguiled? Disperse and unite, when the time is right. In this case, upon a train. In this place, arranged.

Let me climb into this hole behind such illumination, where the views are surreal, but reveal the empty chambers in this roulette, and the one, vague silhouette hidden in a loaded chamber. That which secrets itself, divides between yin and yang and the hand that turns an obscure card.

To fully arrive is to completely let go. Release the hand that must show the one. To the parities and disparities, to the first and the last. If I am allowed to *see* future past and half-stopped at eternal *now*.

Climb in and look out. Hole behind a star. I see that silhouette moving. I see how its card is charaded and guarded from those who might see. And I see the afterglow moon-dial reflected into the eyes of a cruel smile, the never that was ever meant to be.

*I*t is a fairytale moon descends too soon. A kiss goodnight in this afterlight, as the turn and creased beginnings taper and space, disturbed ringings placed as detail upon a ducted bluff. And all is enough and enough is for all as we are slowly scrolled top to bottom and bottom to top, in the prayer that this is just not enough. And all is framed and picture paned and windowed round, presented to there and beyond. It is time. The time has come. It is time. The two are one and yet plotting back against every move. As the king is castled and the queen diagonals to check the rook. As if the all could last forever. As if every tremble and break – for God's sake – could move so much as an atom.

Anyway.

Here we are.

Fairytale moon.

Hole behind a star.

Looking down upon what we are. Not dead, but apart; separated from the end, diversioned from the start.

Here we are.

A kiss from our crescent moon. The silhouette below pretends a sickly tune whistled in a gentle breeze between doors half-open, winking as if (softly spoken) to guide us onto the corrected path. Push the doors wide open. Force them apart. Every beating heart starts between opened doors, for fear they might close again.

Cloaked and reaper grim, I see it matched and motioned toward the erosion of every rock. I see it running the dust through boned fingers, the hearse as it lingers beside the grave, hoping to save half a fraction of a thimbleful of dust.

Taroted, the hanged man corrects against death, altering change. Alas, to withdraw such as they are. Cups and wands turn and bow to the here and eternal now.

It waits and tarries longer, dallies among the lost souls. Checking as it goes.

But that is not all. For as sure as temples fall and churches are abandoned to the wind, there is a change of steer and stirring and a goodness earning stars in a darkening sky.

Yang and Yin meet without and toward within. Spin threads between the strings of perambulation. Turn the emptied bed covers back again.

The tolling bell casts a spell, levelled and retarded, echoing between the unturretted towers that grow higher every day, grow wider and hide all the things we have discarded, grow with every mystery and wish we have ever dreamed or seemed to have begun. Such that cannot be unstopped. These carry on under spells of their own.

S o –
        The horses are racing.

The dead are erasing every step.

Yet the rook is recording and saving and everything is kept.

The slept have awoken.

They shuffle across this coil.

They force their eyes to open, uncertainly loyal to the darkness and that which feasts within. Its mantle pinned to every corner; north, east, south, and west. Feigns to offer harbour for those broken marionettes. But beneath that cloak that kaleidoscopes every grey and deceptive black, the swirls and twirls are neatly unfurled, augmented and randomly exact.

So –

The horses are racing.

The dead know of no regret.

The rook hides among secrets.

The slept have awoken.

But close their eyes again.

Inner voices have spoken.

And they curl up in their sheltering, helter-skeltering slide into void. Awoken, broken and decoyed. And now it's alas to sleep, God rest every soul to keep, every little eye shut tight.

I see all this, from here looking down; above the rook, challenged to join the horses escaping ahead of the hounds that havoc hell, the turns of this carousel, riderless, haunting white dress, taunting back into the bottomless well. Beckoning and reckoning the stop and start of it all. Pulled and reared, their heads are steered, circled around and around, paying their toll upon each revolution. Their stirrups are empty, the saddles ridden by ghosts (their whispers float down to those who will listen). The escapees back to their prison.

So –

(anyway)

We all pay our fee unto the dead, as we remake the beds and turn down the sheets, and the streets are emptied as more come to rest, other guests tired for sleep, submerged far below, sleep to sleep, hands held softly-so.

The storm hurries on, levelled against the wrongs we have undone, thundering against the towers that run endlessly away; hidden, best left hidden, time to pray for our prayers delivered safely there.

But, bear with me a little longer, as it is difficult to explain. Hear me out as I reach to twist my fingers into a mane and ride ahead of a storm that will surely kill one of us – the universe unfolds. The two of us cannot hold and not let go.

It is so.

It is as such as can ever be – this you and me – this lost and found, but never found, only lost and left (as you might have guessed).

Please bear with me a little while yet. There is so much to explain (and yet) so simple a thing to see.

You and me.

A leap toward the moon.

Bride and the groom.

Hands held together.

Stretched here forever.

Looking up through closed eyes.

All those reddening skies blown and pulled away. The mane in my fingers. Raced away. Haste away. A chased away bride.

I am here.

Where are you now, my love?

Your fingers laced into mine.

Have passed in time.

Here, divided between the lines of a broken web.

Subsided beneath the oceans that ebb under a waxing moon, waning loom, weaving all the lines together, lunar collage, counting the stars, never and ever combine and sever, entwine without and within, pencilled and stencilled, then smeared again.

Shh!

Silence.

Shh!

It is over.

Back to the beginning again.

Back to where time began.

Back to where seconds ran one after the other, and minutes and hours gathered pace and days raced like that river toward the sea. You and me.

Shh!

We have peeked between the slats, through the pin holes and plaits. Seen the workings and mechanisms of this and that and the space between atoms where time collects and decants and the dance spins merrily on.

Almost.

No clues in its wake.

All is dissolved and washed away.

Could ever towers crumble and all be gone? All the secrets lost twirling into empty space? Not a trace of a word we shared? The *everything* has been repaired. And Whisperer returns to the palace of death, with his sacks of dust and thimblefuls pushed into the halls of the blessed and forgotten.

Almost.

Except you are not there.

We are not awake.

Whilst the world – the universe – recontinues.

And the oceans break waves upon broken shores. In haste, I might add, for tarry they not, time is always short.

Where are you my love?

Where am I?

Holding hands.

Remembering a kiss.

That became all this.

Because a whisperer.

Made this happen.

Then disappeared.

You!

We!

Overstepped the mark.

You made out to listen.

But you did not.

Took me with you.

And now we are lost.

Oh – dear – God!

I must climb down now.

The webs have closed.

But in this world or that world, or whichever, or whatever the thread, wherever or whenever that web – I will find you.

Silvered and spattered, moon and stars scattered across a hooded hemisphere. Uncountable. Infinity and eternity are, of course, one and the same. Trailing fan-tailed, thrown snipered-snipering galaxies over tall ships sailing a fallowed breeze upon displaced polarities.

Here is where they run aground. The roar of wood and sea and sand and rush upon a shallow beach, behind a reflected-deflected tide, sliding along the horizonless sky. Diamonds glint upon the tip of every wave. Worthless, yet precious jewellery cobalt blue and surely swathes and ricochets play. Crazed and stirred from far and deeper below.

Yet the moon pulls the earth to a kiss it cannot reach, warps the oceans dragged to every beach. Runs along, along and then upon every grain of sand expanded into its each peculiar world, every tiniest a cosmos unto itself. Every shiniest diamond a sparkle in the effervescent stealth of fizz and foam. And home might be in a moment in any one of these.

Yet the moon not always the night delivers. Often lost by visible suns, midday and morning runs. Though, blushed evenings are best and midnights even better still. She cradles her crisp arrival, her skills of continued survival; kisses and smiles.

And the sun heeds no better. Yet more reliable than Madam Moon. Desolates, eradicates, every flux caught in the loom that snaps and traps destinies like here – merely a lonely place for souls to divide.

And what of heaven, my love?

And what of hell?

And the opposite to which opposite is not?

And what of angels, my love?

Do they steer our ragged ships?

Or bury them here, with a kiss?

Deliver our souls or leave them lost, wandering between the stars, the moon, and the sun. These impatient duties washed clean away and allowed no return. Washed in the sea, dried in a breeze, crumbled into the tide; all the sailors died this day – and next.

Hence to try and make sense of these forsaken thoughts. Smoke and mirrors, saviours and killers, chance and trickery when there is no chance at all. Preordained, this fate we blame for every suspicion, zig-zag snagged, good and bad, everything that never was, everything we never had.

I know these things.

And I know it is not too late.

I need to focus.

To bring myself awake.

I know of that.

And I know of this.

I can still feel you.

Upon my lips.

(I taste you on my lips, too)
So, gone are the horses.
Waiting as we left.
As we leapt – I was holding onto you.
And you – holding onto me.
Told to deliver us.

Pausing all the clocks.

But they were too high above.

How could we and fortune evoke and reveal this love unlike any parade or serenade, made-to-measure forever? How could we displace the fixed face that hides behind silhouettes and tethers and ties and oh, so many lies? How could we rely on a wish? There was no other way than this!

I am here. Entangled, too. Not so very far from you. Not so very far away. And you are right, of course,, it is the 'and' in random that realigned the source of ours and every line. For that specific micro moment, atom of atomic time, we shifted and stopped the pendulum clocks and click tik-toks, locking and unlocking with the dust of the dead.

I passed over, my love.

But you linger still.

Life holds onto you.

Against your will.

Cruel and ungodly.

But we are still *entwined.*

The remote ruffle and rimple of time encloses our love and sparks every line that ran ahead, every rhyme, everything we said – I swear, your rook has not left us yet.

If you can hear me.

Be patient a little while longer.

I seek that phantom that believes is stronger, along there is a special place for you and I. The maze of whispers is misshapen and snarled. It hobbles and topples, dry lips into dry dust. Screwed black eyes, chained to its lies and deceit. It rises, open handed and golden with a light to follow that we may meet. Duplicity! Yin and Yang. Sometimes combined and whole and one.

But they have an enemy, my love.

A weakness only we have found.
Hobbling and toppling to the ground.
Be patient yet, my love.
We shall always *be true.*
Be patient, my love.
And I will find you.

K ing of kings. I weave every web. I structure and make a place for the dead. I allow this universe to spin and for stars to collide. I do not need to justify. Let my good light guide you – but keep the darkness close beside you. Decide what you believe. I lie – but I do not deceive.

S aw me, perhaps, in that hole behind a star. But ignored me, perhaps, knowing who we are. Left me, indeed, to this chimera disease where every word dissolves a fantasy. Left me, I suppose, saddened – that this had ever happened, had ever seen a flaw in the perfect web. Not I. She will strum the chords of endless symmetry whilst I ponder and wonder at all this. Words are only doodles and squiggles to draw around the riddles of this and what has ever been. The sum of the total. The clues of the immortal. The dreams we have woven, letters burned unopened. The screams and cries surpressed. Sum of total. Abandon the rest (if you wish – secrets) (then, keep them to yourself).

I hear you my love.

Saw me, no doubt, from its chambered roulette. Loaded and rode its bullet, reset, waiting for a hammer to strike and a trigger to pull and put it all right.

Saw and ignored me – as I looked down from that star. Too far away to interfere. Yet every thread draws everything near.

The sound of one hand clapping (they say) is the rhythm you will hear if you are on the way, not lost, but corrected path. For it is that upon which every bubble prevails, before the first and beyond the last. Every cocoon and shell and chrysalis fell onto textures of lesioned lawns, kicked and rolled as freedom called and crawled crawling, new form awakened.

Oh, butterfly in a jar.

Taken from your flight. To flutter and flitter torn wings skittered and folded away. To bluster and blister, twisted behind the glass. Upside down in your mist where you stick, colours of dust against your kissed jar – because you are – so beautiful. You are so undisputedly sublime to that dream (of freedom contained). So exactly aligned to all that has already been preordained.

We are the same.

For Gods's sake.

Broken winged and too late to follow the sun, because, once more, the moon is arriving. This time upon an evening. Smiling. Fairytales colliding. Gliding from glass down to earth. Colours powdered behind you, dust for what dust is worth.

We were playing, That was all. Chasing such butterflies and (in the evening fireflies) capturing them in our hearts. You were saying – a storm is on its way. (was this before or after the kiss?)(before the first and beyond the last).

Absurd or not, we tarry and cast these charms. We crouch and presume to collate hidden heavens, obvious hells; amble, but never wait. Our sums are checked, correct, profits and holes in pockets. A ferryman's toll to the other side. *And if you be short there be no port to receive you!'*

Black onto black, ridiculous that we might continue in this way.

Look!!!

Storm clouds gather.

The clouds are

like horses –

running away.

Don't be afraid.

Your kiss has made this.

No, it hasn't.

Yes, it has.

Kiss me again!.

And we run as if every turn might unleash a beast. As least, pieced into our re-jigged sky. No time to decide.

'Ha! Ha!'

Run as if we could fly!

Run and run.

The storm has come.

As if we could die!

'Ha! Ha!'

I unfold here. Sentences and paragraphs unroll here. Words – mushroom into irrelevance. Intelligence fades and angles away. Indifference and nothingness in everything we say. Every symbol and dot, every table and chart – pulls – pulls my heart apart. Scream inside all these phrases, divide and divide again. They crimp upon every hem, pull, arise, and descend.

Cold here. Numbness steeps into every bone. And yet I am unable to die. The shadows scuffle slowly forward, moving toward the graves of regretful sighs. All those lives – hap-hazzard and gone. All that has left arrives. All that is gone has gone and gone away.

I would close my closed eyes, clench my fists and cry out to God. I would! I would! I would pull back my lips and stare-eyed into blue skies. I would shake and agitate and rattle every bone. I would scream so loud, like the world has never known. I would scream – lost in the scheme of unschemed nothings.

But, by and by, nothing is everything, in fact. Draw my mind back. Beyond that first kiss. Beyond that first storm. White dress soaked and worn sopped to skin, a beginning, born within a moment unwoven into the web.

Steal a kiss – and now move on.

Years are none and gone away. Nothing else to remember. Only that day and somebody's wedding day and a train that fades toward honeymoon. The afternoon, wine and time wrapped one around the other as features and fields and worlds unreal speed lovers, discover discovered and discovered again. Racing through a land of summer green, seen through our window; barns and hedges and grasslands and denes, farms and woodlands and meadows teem, dotted with colour, fuller deep greens emerging, yellows and blues converging.

I remember all this.

The turn of a key.

You sat in front of me.

I remember in white.

Softest hue.

I remember you saying

I do.

I remember that moment.

So close to my heart.

Uneraseable, unfadeable, inescapably mine and yours, yours and mine; glasses raised with wine.

'It is beautiful,' I say

(was that a wink?)

You will *remember this day*.

'Like the day we first kissed.'

'*Yes*.'

Like the day we first wished we could climb among the stars and the universe would be ours.

'*Yes*.'

Like the storm that tied us close when you arose to kiss me back. I remember that. A run against your skin. Running. Dripping down your neck. Soaking wet. Thundering up above. Lightening our love. Striking, corroding, and rusting and blasting to spatters every molecule that might stand between us. Like that?

'Yes.'

I remember the moment.

So close to my heart.

Then, take my hand.

And follow me.

It was the moon beginning. And the horses had gathered to bring the storm in. And the shadows had mustered, clustered our stars into clouds. Had roused the reds and garnets and maroons ahead of the cymbols, clashes and booms that would quake and break horizons.

The world would end. Or so it would seem. But you had your mind on other things.

'Then, take my hand, husband.'

'You will remember this day.'

And I remember it well as yet; our walk to that door, as the train rushed forward, and we balanced and kept our hands held tight. I remember your face. Sweet. White. Amazing graces laced and light strobing every shadow. I remember (so close). I remember (closer than close). You look into my eyes. As we walk toward that door. As you hold me once more. Pull me close – the dice cubed and cast. This is the first. And this is the last. We can both be *truly* free!

'I love you!'

And the clasp clicks open.

'I love you!'

King of Kings. The webs are all rewoven. I raise my lantern, burning in an empty hall. The joy of it all. The bride before the fall. The towers are not so clear now, now our rook has off'd away. (The lantern flickers as the hall expands and the doors open for another day).

This, as you know, is my responsibility; to ensure each day follows the next. You will also know, every seam is checked and repaired should love decide to unhook a thread. Or, perhaps, having listened to my whispers where I have allowed gaps and cracks and evening skies to red. This is where I can audience the dead, host to the ghosts and turn down their beds. This is where spirits are rallied and queue by the stairs labelled nirvana and I am able to open their eyes as we play out this drama. Not dead at all, just gently sleeping, dimensioned into my safe keeping. Not dead at all, empty halls are full of unseen ghosts. If I raise my lantern a little higher you may see where each shadow cloaks a hidden flame. No two the same. Each burning a dance of light in the darkness. Turning circles to mark this and every hole behind every star.

This you may not know, is my duty also, to flow every river to its source, every ocean to the cause and regret never found among the towers of collected moments and words. Piled and buried with the have and have never heards. I blow them down, every one into dust, collected and carried and rushed to the bottom of the bottomless sea by rivers – because only rivers are free. This I allow. Unimprinted from the webs. That they may follow, as they will, a destiny of their own. No other energy needs to be unchained – each must follow its line, because each river will deliver each little flame to mine.

All of this is all it is. It *is* all there is. There are no uncertainties or disparities. All is as it could only ever be. I merely ensure this, control this; because what you see is nothing more than illusion. But, in fact, *something* moves in its mysterious ways; plays the days and destinies for the numbers that roll off the dice. *Something* to entice with a whisper, might tempt you to pull over and kiss her.

Are such moments free, do you think? Or wound and threaded with a wink? 'Of course they are.'

Only the rivers run free, as I say – Oh, and I forgot to mention, the *rook*, too, by the way. Free to collect what it believes needs keeping. Reaping what has been sown, ripping what has been sewn – and that by a turn of a card.

This, you *really* should know; I cancel light with darkness and night with day. I roll the earth around the sun in a universe inbetween every one and every one is off and on, in and out, right and wrong. I am every one and every one is me. Can't you see? I *am He.*

A murmer oars across to twist a curved whisper from this vista of marooned drumming. A wound running crosswise, coming disguised to the cut of a burning knife. The murmer besets an energy. Like a choir rising crescendo. The vaulted vaults echo and ring to the halts, the stops, and starts – and every soul departs at the foot of the stairs. Descends or ascends, swears allegiance to Off or On, also known as Each and Everyone.

Along the corridors, toward a hall of a trillion, trillion, trillion wicks, each waiting to be lit. It is here – your final decision – will she or won't she listen?

Whisperers script has already been prepared. Checked and authenticated and shared, doors about to be unlocked. Take a position. Behind a leaf, a log, a grain, any one of a countless drops of rain – waiting for the storm.

Curtain up!

A bow, 'For your pleasure.'

Forever is, in deed, a long time waiting.

Here they come! Running through the trees. Tussled and ruffled in the July breeze. Here they come! Laughing aloud, scuffed at the knees, browned by the sun, between dapples that burn soft yellows that murmur and rattle, hazed oranges that settle in the leas of these aquamarines and ragged greens.

Here they come. Here they arrive. Puffed and dizzied, their cries rising into happy skies, feet sinking into the embrace of cool, shallow pools, luring, pulling them to the ground. Pulling to be found. Fallen into the grass. Pulled to the sound, hushed as hearts beat, resonate and pound. Pulled to the invisible voice hidden among the leaves. And behind all of these, beneath buried rocks, within hollow logs, and raindrops and grains and gritted remnants, the audience await in awe.

There they lie. And laugh and kick and roll. There they sigh and loudly go. There they crawl – two commandos moving into the weeds, lying on their backs, beads in broken webs.

It is then, to her, Whisperer said,

'A storm is about to break.

For your sake

You must leave now.

Horses are unleashed

You will see them allow

Black into a blood red sky.'

A mirror-imaged flare divides and converges and severs beasts from lair. This team; these mares, hooves thundering in escape, flashing as they break and legion astral armies in their wake. This team arrows lightening, gathers fanfares, striking a frightened world.

'The storm is faraway

But comes quickly.

Quicker than you think.

Do not hesitate.

There is a lie concealed

Behind every blink.'

This moment a portal opens all destinies are broken. This moment is only that. Just enough. That is this and that is also. Curtains opened as threads and webs are severed, cleared and quickly respun again. This portal so brief. It is here among the leaves, window opened wide, he looks into her eyes, smell her breath, taste her voice, "Is it a branch from a tree?"

"Not any old tree! It's a supernatural tree."

"Of course."

Touches her lips with his.

"Oh!"

"Invisible, did you say?"

"Was that a kiss?"

But already too late. The dead look on. The rook hovers high, high above. The webs are rewoven and all back in place – besides one, single thread – missing.

Audience looks on.

Whisperer responds, hissing as a whisperer would.

Rook flies on beneath the hood of a tinting sky.

Horses arrive.

Too late to save the day.

Too late to delay.

Blood red.

Once again, the heat of the day scrapes blades, cutting into the parched earth. Burns out the sundials, murmurs another curse. Once again, eyes unopened, her hand in mine. Again – withered and unaligned to this eternal time. Scissored and ragged, wrung and snagged, clipped, stripped and shredded. Every moment colossus, raise your tall crosses, raise and erase, burn them down again. This heat of the day. This hand held in mine. This line that is no line seems to run on forever. This sum adds minus to zero, subtracts and squares above and below, within and without, and there remains no doubt this all runs on into nothing. What kind of sum? What kind of sun? Would add nothing, yet burn eternal?

Hand in my hand.

Where are you now, my love?

silence

Do I merely wait to rise upon my passing and find you there? Or will this wheel turn forever?

silence

Or – do I need to remember – something? A key to unlock all of this?

I seem only allowed these few contrary, disordered memories.

Is it hidden in one of these?

And would I know if I found it?

The heat cycles and turns that turning wheel. Intensity. The immensity of it all. The seventh seal – waits. Pandora delegates the decision. The sun is at its zenith, here endeth the lesson, the final finality, the broken polarity of every atom that threw an electron into a higher orbit. The rook saw it and, in short while, added it to another pile.

White.
Soaked white.
Running ahead of the storm.
Racing ahead of those horses.
Running and running.
Black.
Deepest black.

Born of the causes and creations.
The lines and deviations.
The race to home.
We.
Born to be together.
Never and un-never.
Whether, if ever, if ever or not.
We should dance as the sky cracks.
And lightening fuses.
And you turn – and kiss me back.
'It is beautiful,' I say.
(forever mine) *'Then, take my hand.'*

And we dance to our beds where nothing is said and nothing revealed, sealed with the softest kiss. Never meant to be.

Just thee and me.

Swizzled and entangled, destined and reangled, currents that have lost their way, horizons fazed between here and there. World out of focus, we crawl through the maze to find finality. But there is none to find. Blindfolded. The signs lead to nowhere. Beholding and beholded, pointed and anointed, wedged we are, betwixt, between every hole behind every star. Threads they are. Ours removed and without a turn, we run (as we ran from the rain), without no more or less from thee, or me; without a line, without hindrance. Free (if you see what I mean), but without a current to take us. Without a future to shape us.

Did we *really* leap from there to here directly?
Did we *really, really* arrive like this?
Was there nothing inbetween?
Nothing between the memories.

Rushed and pushed. Because finales were unmatched and required resolution. Solution. No key.

Illusions, you see!

Confusion spills and whirlpools in swamps dilated once and for all, draws and pulls as we rock and we roll, sucks and swallows all our tomorrows. Plucks and follows our dreams and sorrows, tucks every hope into its deepest recess. Hidden and lost, resets the stopped clocks.

Tik-Tok.

Tik-Tok.

Unable to stop. Spring fully wound.

Hearts pound.

Tik-Tok.

Tik-Tok.

Loud.

Crowned.

- King Of Kings.

Lantern allied.

How high the rook flies.

And seeks.

Any measure of this.

Did we really leap from there to here directly?

Nothing inbetween.

Just church.

And train.

After we ran through the rain?

And the sky cracked.

And lightening fused.

And you kissed me back.

Oh – dear – God.

Sky is above thee.

To a church.

Again, dressed in white.

Again, the most beautiful white.

Again, light precedes the darkness. As one less feature divides past between present, mashed into all and lessened and the sums renumbered and wished away.

There was never *anything* inbetween.

Rejoined the threads.

Criss-crossed everything that might have been, jumped over every single moment, pushed our energies into a stream that ran free into the sea, every ocean as these, too, run free. Every (key) of thee and me. Every (key) that was never meant to be.

And so it is as it is and was. Elaborate the every cause that held onto lost beginnings and middles as endings all unite, all pending realities suffice, all threads, (only ours) spliced and abridged.

We enter from woodland through an alleyway between nothing and nothing, our tunnels crossing, avoiding weighted drops, because here the clocks never started or stopped. We arrive at a church, searching for where we are. Our exit behind a star (dream sequence) as we await (low frequence) as children at the centre of infinity. Suddenly adults (such expedience!) before divinity, pronounced as man and wife.

'For the rest of your life.'

'I love you.'

'I love you.'

Dressed in white.

'It's the same dress!'

Behind us the exit has closed.

Our threads retied.

'*I see it now!*'

Rushed through.

Me and you.

Children in a wood, storm, red skies and rain renewed. Overviewed. Clued in and lined in and scored out. Diverted in, finding, and found out.

Because of whispers in your ear.

(what did you hear?)

Because of a kiss.

(what did He say?)

(before the kiss.)

(before far and near converged, and up and down, around and around emerged and underground and overground wound in the breaths and sighs, turned away the eyes that looked but could not see. Turned, revised misdirection, a displaced projection to here.)

I see it now.

At the beginning at the end of all days.

At once we have become of age.

'I love you.'

Man and wife.

'*I love you.*'

'Invisible,' I said.

almost

'Invisible indeed!'

And we are running between platforms for tickets on stations unknown, stamped *journey*, clipped; surely far from home. Trains and great windows and blurred where the wind blows and daubs the slightest rouge for your rewards.

This is overlap of lines.
Raise our glasses.
As time rewinds for you and I.
This *is* the *same* sky.
Here come the horses!
Those whispers in your ear.
What did you hear?
What did He say?
What did you do!

Illuminations smoulder, grow colder and fade, sparkle and snuffle everything laid out and divined, designed and displayed and purposefully mis-signed. Follow the clues that lead you to nowhere; simple to follow, straight and clear. Except (as you know) no line is straight and fate and all we deserve, bends and shifts to every curve.

So – What did I hear? What did He say? And what did I do? I heard prayers and despairs. I heard there were stairs. He would meet me there. I heard it was time to move quickly, for a storm coming would lift me and carry me to a place. Horses arrive to race me away. All I had to do was grace Him with a kiss.. But you kissed me instead. Our threads, my love, were not repaired. The impurity of another's kiss, meant this. This. This. Where we are now. All those others – the others that died – brides, my darling. Trillions and trillions and trillions – of brides.

Alas, the curved lines helix and twist, you must remember this – they exist, wound around His black heart. Yet, as surreal as this may seem: a light brightens the black, lightens those cracks

that run jagged and keep us apart. His heart is a lantern that
swings in an empty hall. He holds it high, protects us all. X-rays
and sees through every thought. X-reads and totals and exposes
every short. Underlines the sums that distort and report lies as
truths. For truths (as you also know) are usually untrue.

    Anyway, my love.
    Do not be afraid.
    You must wait for me.
    For I know more than I can say.
    Because.
    What did I do?
    Why – back – I kissed you.
    And that is enough.
    For now.

Blindfolded and masked, alas, yes, miraged and riveted below every eve, bizarre and levitated we arise and are conceived. Crimped and buckled, deceived, unbelieved and sweet sugar sprinkled. We are as we are or could ever have been. Every knot pulled tight. Every uncensored dream. Every forgotten plot in this runaway stream. As the last voice dies from the crescendo choir, the rook alights from his tall sunspire – swoops and loops over vista and plain, ahead of storms, ahead of trains. Higher than the highest heaven known to God, beyond and beyond this odd and most peculiar symmetry of parallels and diversions. The servants look on as the congregation *cracks* silent and the alignments are trimmed and the murmers dwindle away. The dead return to their belated greys and blacks and monochrome flats. Some will down and some will up. The stairs clatter as the just and the corrupt select their steps and the bluffed will be bluffed again.

Ever higher.

Your heart's desires.

Higher and higher.

Our free spirit wings where wings will take him.

Unreadable.

Unknowable.

Collecting.

Selecting and building those columns out of all those forgotten means. Even kings and queens and as such as all those might have been – but never were.

Piling them tall, for fear they might fall and bury the world beneath all those forgotten things. For fear they might wobble and topple at the restlessness of the dead and their sins and the strings, pulled tight.

This flight.

This passage above the web.

Searching for the line, the cut away thread.

The discarded undestiny of one who is dead.

And one who is waiting to die.

Such a jewel.

Worthy of the highest tower.

This thread unfulfilled, freewilled nothing.

This finally stilled missed crossing.

Lost, it would seem. Perhaps buried deep. Deeper than the dead. Perhaps hidden, unreachable, below the bed of the sea?

But nothing is unreachable.

And nothing unseemable.

For the collector seeking truth.

Because – *really* – the skeletons dance in their gateway, perchance to the rhythm of dry, bleached bones. They click and clack and crumble and snap and are collected and stacked like stones; piled and crushed into the finest dust. They are released, in this sense; a deliverance, to blow and disperse, last to first, all into none, and none into *one*.

Because – *really* – the constellations entwine, diverge and design, oblique to the lines that run beyond touching distance. The swirl of the stars and solar systems; countless and limitless; but nevertheless, totalled in this infinite sum.

Because – *actually* – from stars and stardust every bone has been crafted. Every eye that counted from a star's heart mastered that it may look back upon itself.

Because – *actually* – fixed-snake-stare in that moment we make, a hypnotic cosmos turns and turns alike, backs before the strike, earth and moon and stars might, indeed, sum total all this wealth.

And now.

Circling.

Wings spread wide.

Aware.

Every here and there.

Every then and now.

Every wedding vow.

Soars and rises and climbs a dot in the sky. Blinks in and out of every blink of every eye, of every truth and lost 'little lie.'

Higher.

To see back and then.

Before horses released.

Before it all began.

The web as it was.

The cure and the cause.

Counting stars.

That's how it was.

Just two kids, one moon, and a trillion, trillion, trillion stars.

'**S**hh!'

　'Quiet.'

'Listen…'

'Shh.'

'Don't shush. Listen!'

nothing

'Thought I saw a shadow fly over the face of the moon.'

'Me, too…'

silence

'…but I didn't hear it.'

'Me, neither.'

'How many stars did you count?'

'One-hundred-and-fifty-six!'

'Me, too.'

silence

'So that's how many stars there are in the sky.'

'I know. That's a lot of stars.'

C old rolls, pushes its fingers into every nook and every fracture. Captures breath, traces death. Steals in with the night. And the night with a mist were veils before we kissed, allowed, now, to remember this. To suddenly reveal the surreal clarity of it all.

All those stars.

And a moon, besides.

All those stars!

One-hundred-and-fifty-six divides by the square of every darkening sky. Tapped upon the tip of little fingers counting, logging each to its revelry. God would have counted these as well and as well as might and might as well have been. They teem and spill as would swirl and splice. They gleam and run quicker, each dim light flickers – 'Count me again into this night.'

Ahh!

I remember so clearly now.

You run your fingers through your hair.

You sparkle.

I am aware.

Charcoal.

Sketched.

Eyes.

Stare and realise.

We need to recount those stars.

Tomorrow.

Out in the woods alone.

Watch out for that shadow.

Passing over the moon.

First to last. The train runs faster than had been expected then. Beginning to end. Destinations pretend to almost arrive. But arrival, alas, rushes on past. No names, only places, no places, no stops. No here or there, or anywhere. No thought of resequenced webs or overlapping threads, cut and short-circuited to here. No thought of anything, except me and thee and the nearness of another storm.

Glasses raised to this change in the weather.

Chink!

You and me.

Forever and ever.

Where are you now, my love?

Rushed running ahead, this second day treads tip-toe below a lattice sky. This butterfly effect of you and I dissects and slides. Jam jars and fireflies, unbeknown to those now sleeping (in their safe havens), safe keeping, curled and furled, awaiting the eve, as we do; believing as we do, our stars readied for the counting; the backdrop universe discounting every one.

This is before the lines and circles and hearts. This is before the storm, and before the sun departs. This is as children play. Before the horses and whisperers and dead audiences watched us spin away. Spin and spin and spin indeed. Away and away. Allowed and loosened, cut free from the web, destiny ebbs and sheds lock-linked chains.

This is how it was. This is how a kiss began. Because we are entangled polarities of yin and yang. The kiss which meant to enslave you became another kiss, erased you and laced you back into the threads; these repairs patched and matched to exactly that which honeycombs into definitely not – slots – closed to every single deed. This is that which stains, but cannot see. This is that, as that is this – shh! (it was the gentlest kiss).

Looking, but imprismed in this horror, withdrawn and retiring in your honour. The kiss-back turn turning the ghosts upon themselves. Trillioned feet, I swear, deprived and torn. Demure and lured, skewered and contrasted below the storm. The flash and flicker and quickly retreat, pull away the disguise and lairs, rush-rushing, fleeting toward those stairs and bluffs and huffs and puffs and such stuff as ghosts are made of.

The turn-back kiss.

But, before all this.

We had gathered ourselves this day to count the stars. No distractions, additions or subtractions; just us awaiting the dark, climbing through fields and running in trees, July sun, skin-burned, squeezed between every blade of grass and broken branch and entrance into every other world.

Skyline shifts.

Horizons lift.

Hearts and circles and spells and truths before the face of God. Your horses released. Your carriage prepared for your place on the stairs, to your venue awaiting appointment. Bride of He, excorcised – because you kissed me back.

And on! Horses away!

Too late!

To fulfil their role.

The hounds run on noisily, then noiselessly behind them. Snarled, teeth bared, razored red, but vacant in their following, silenced, empty muting in the tombs and catacombs of echoes. Lost – for they have missed their bride.

Yet the stars are in need of counting. Before all these dark beginnings. Each one placed and spaced, spinning and spindled – illuminating as we count them one by one. Brightening as we link arms and rest upon a singleness of our own.

"One-hundred-and-fifty-six!"

"You were right."

See how bright they spark into life as soon as they are counted! See how swirled and illusioned, pearled and fused and curled and excused from eternity they are accounted. Zero plus zero to the square of none, every single nothing trillioned to none. Trillioned, trillioned, and trillioned again. There is only One.

"One-hundred-and-fifty-six!"

"I'll say! That's a lot of stars."

"I know."

"I can see them – tiniest specks of the universe sprinkled into your eyes."

I can say this now. You would have smiled and pinched me then. Rolled away. Turned away. Laughing.

I miss you, my love.

Need you.

I did! I saw every zero star shining in your eyes. I did!

But, one-hundred-and-fifty-six, then, were a lot of stars.

Until the shadow passed across the moon.

Raise my lantern that little higher. That I may lift the wire and oversee these endless candles, rooted to the web of angles, angled out again and back upon themselves. These souls under my keeping, sleeping deep in the safety of their sleep.

Raise and lower, that the shadows may show her that which she gave away, lost for the price of a kiss. See this! How you were planned in, fortuned and webbed in from the very beginnings of time. Foolish you to *chink* your wineglasses and stop the clocks, stop the wheels, clog the cogs, seal the passages, all that matters is.....it is too late to turn back time.

Raise and praise where praise is due. He lies there searching, but is right there next to you. The web is matted and patched. And for that I must make as best I can. Shorted from then to now with no inbetween. But I offered you a wedding; because that love was true. And truly as true as truest can be – it was. Alas, however, here or wherever, never destined to be again. I am also the lantern by which all shadows are cast, light before and dark behind . Light and darkness, bride and groom, life prevails before loom and filament.

Overseer am I.

Masquerades and hushed parades.

Arrow drawn.

Bullet placed into its chamber.

Under here am I.

Tunnelled and funnelled.

Cross-wired and jumbled.

To a church perched upon where-wherever, spectred and dreamed, composed that your scene might allow second chance. Honeymoon train. Objection sustained and allowed your partial forever. But the hounds that drive the horses force you to pause this moment before the stars. For your stars are numbered, just so your moon may slumber a sleepy sigh.

And where be I?

Waiting!

You *promised* me!

You whispered back –

'Allow him to be free.'

'Catch a horse, dearest!' Is that what I said?

How dare you smile and not comfort Me as all destinies are rethreaded?

'I take that as a *yes.'*

(only silence)

'Do I have a choice?'

(only silence)

'Then, the horses will, once again, be loosed that you may join Me.'

'Allow him to be free.'

'Of course. But you must catch a horse to find me.'

(only silence)

'They are already being driven by the hounds. Make sure you catch as you rise, but don't look down.'

(only silence)

'They will be with you quicker than you think. The hounds of hell drive furiously that I may close this final chapter.'

Is that how it was?

No cure.

No cause.

Oh – dear God – do I address Myself?

To whom *do* I address?

I am still here; negated below an evaporating sun. This one, at least the fourth turn around our capsized world. The groom returns as I lose count of the elliptical circles. The bride departs as the final star sparkles – the moon one-quarter full. The uncrossed gather to pay their toll. Motionless, dead-still, I await my call – just the roll of a dice over a down-turned card, yet the spirit of neverness as an assassin guards and keeps, no release until faced up – if ever.

Show your hand that I may mine. Raise the stakes. Raise the wine. What is it to be feared? Lost and unaccounted. Your thread of time? Betrayed, perhaps? The kiss was mine and never Yours. Howbeit I can lie here, a hazy blueprint of schemes and intrigues, when your jealousy allowed the laws of fate to twist and pause and stop this purer love?

I cannot lie here forever.

We cannot be divided as between days and nights.

Cannot.

Cannot.

Cannot.

Darkness and light belong to the moon and the stars, phases and changes, enhanced to become one. Is this remote drift to be undone? Is this undoing also to be added to none?

As sure as chaos and reason announce modest disparity, so confusion and illusion denounce their clarity.

Hence the hearts, circles, and lines. Hence the clues and disjointed rhymes and chimes from unwound clocks, stopped at the point of the great undoing. How can this be so?

I await, as you ask, my love.

I believe there is a key to a door.

My heart still beats, my lungs slowly fill, drawing air into my blacked out world. My pulse prevails. My senses dulled. My body splayed, fades, but pulled back to the greyed margins that curl back from the ethereal. My stillness and silence concealed in a hole behind a star, in a pit, is that where *we* are? Fallen together in this foreverness we call our own?

How do I know this?

How can it be so?

I await, as you ask, my love.

The door through which every soul must pass counts in the first and counts out the last.

You are the key, my love.

Future imperfect, past, present and cast across fortune's table.

Turn that card over! That I may see its face.

Turn it yourself. Before it is erased.

The dice has turned a second six. Could be destiny has allowed this?

A second card? *Come on!*

And another card is turned.

How am I to play against destiny? How can this be? How can it be so?

I await, as you ask, my love.

Turn the card!

Before it is erased.

First and second card opening.

For what were you hoping?

Back!

Back in our wood.

Before the storm.

Before the kiss.

Before all of this.

Then turn the cards! First and last. First and second. As each soul walks past. Count them in and count them out, count them through, there is no doubt – every one, just as every star, is counted and summed to total.

I turn it, but do not recognise the face. Second card is the face of the first, placed and reversed, top-tailed and inversed. Distorted. Convexed and cankered, it splits the embrace, separated and shuffled back into the deck.

Take another and concede your soul.

You may draw from the pack a trillion fold.

You may raise another journey and another train.

You will *never* see her again!

Glittery gliding as the omniverse is sliding resplendent across the night. Specked and spangled, unevenly triangled and squared entangled into the web.

The circles surrounding everything in there. Invisibled and ghosted, spirited closest to that within. For within is without as the tendrils and webs stretch into every conceivable corner. I know this. Taunted. Haunted. Centred, ground zero, pin-pointed.

Fortunes cards are a trickery. Just as the dice rolls quickly across the table. Too fast to see. Too blurred, glazed and fogged to be anything but a lie. Those cubed spots spin as they ride, wheel and hide any tiniest absolute truths.

Yet I await, as you ask, my love.

Growing late now.

Every single star of ours waits now.

Every breath in the death of life abates now.

Everything.

Everything dissipates.

Feel I am falling away.

Here.

Circled star and invisibled we touch.

I love you.

There are not enough storms.

I *love* you.

Not enough dawns, or mornings, or red sky warnings.

I trust you.

I believe your horses are waiting.

I am ready to leave now.
Ahead of the hounds that bark hungrily at our heels.

I love you, too.

I can hear the bells tolling as the pack is reshuffled, the first kissed and the dice pitched across the darkness.

Be ready!

Think of black. Now treble that. Now multiply it by a zillion. Add a zillion and measure it as half a grain of sand. Now, step back as far as you can and as far as you can see, dunes and deserts of dust and disease. Further back and further back, there is nought to observe, only nothingness and hollowed tomorrows.

Yet this is where I am, and here is where I rest. Only the gentlest sound of my chest. Rises and falls. As if nothing at all could disturb such a faraway sleep.

Rise and fall.

In this hall without a lantern.

Fall and rise.

In this hushed habit of phantoms.

Flicking back.

And flickering forth.

Stammering eddies that have outrun their course.

Deleted whispers return to source on rivers that run free as our causeway ships prepare to voyage beyond the pale of danced horizons.

So be it!

Hoist the sails!

An end of it.

Hoist the sails – and dance!

Come, my love.
Where are the skies of red?
Where is the storm?
The carriage and train?
The rain?
Ready for the leap?
Come, my love.

I need the sky and thunder, all illuminating shadows belly under to hell – come drag it forth, release every beast, light the torches, chant and rise for death's release. Rip out the web from the darkest expanse. Come! Come with us. Come dance the dance to discover – there is not only *One* – there is another!

But the stillness is black.
As I await.
For you.
To come back.
And the black is total voidness.
As I breathe to avoid this.
Silence.
Who is this *other*?

The gatherer of forgotten dreams soars high above the gloom, glides high above the soon to be polarities of Yang and Yin, where it all begins and ends and begins again. Splices and veers, switches and shears, appears and disappears, steers – then reappears between cloud over star – a shadow across the moon. Lifts up, up, and out of sight. Its flight powering and emerging, angled and reverting wing-tip to tail-tip, feathered and ripped, slipping through the sky, pointed and sleek – *something* in its beak. Some *glow* behind black eyes. A purpose to glide down toward the earth.

Down.

Down.

The hearse draws up for its thimbleful of dust, tarries, then hurries away. Today is the same day. Yesterday and tomorrow – tomorrow and tomorrow and tomorrow – petty paced and scooped out like empty skulls, crushed to dust those thimblefuls of recorded time.

Alas – down and down.

Deeper and steeper.

Then around.

Circles into spirals.

Air beneath wings.

Circling.

Corkscrewing.

Down and deeper down.

To that hole of invisible circles.

Almost, behind a star.

Is where they are.

One dead.

One dying.

Holding hands.

Cards and fortune.

Displaced.

Sands spilling through eternal time.

Paused time.

Unjoined.

Awaiting the other's return.
Death to life.
And life to death.
Joined as one.
And down.
Deeper down he glides.
That *something* within his eye.
That *other thing* within his beak.

A nd that I should allow this thing (love) to transcend. Allow and forgive and even begin again.

I think not.
For she rides the lead horse.
Through skies of recourse.
To erase and begin again.
She will repair and fix.
All of this.
She will rescue and release.
That which she must.
This I must trust.
And then come to me.
Only *he.*
Must be freed.
Ha! Ha!
How is that!

How could I not destroy this void of simple emptiness within which he resides? How could I not merely enjoy this beautiful divide? This set aside, this groom and bride – they are children, nothing more.

They are playing.

I knock.

One answers the door.

Ha! Ha!

Children – northing more.

The perfect bride. None of this false hearted need to decide. We are estranged. Yet about to arrive. Come! I await, though I know he survived.

And now.

I am about to let him go.

Clasp the mane tight.

Kick in your heels.

The steady knell.

Cry 'Havoc!'

Release the hounds of hell.

Unleash a savage sky.

Bloodied and hurried, for I allow his release, only that you may return. Watch you dip below the storm, the cherry-crimson abyss, the kiss – you *know* where he is – as you ride the breaks to reach him.

Way ahead and out of view.

Do you think I cannot see you?

As you drop streamlined, trainlined clouds fragmenting, augmenting, lamenting it all. This fall from grace for a single embrace. This sweet sacrifice racing below the storm. Bride and groom torn separate by the veils and shreds and various reds and a death to keep you apart.

Now nearly over. The far rumbles of thunder precede the tolling bell.

Now almost complete, the beating of every heart – stops! Every fleeting moment locks, blocking out the light. Especially star night. Even the sighing moon. Even groom from the eyes of the bride.

Hurry and have this over, I say!

Finish it now.

Even *I* will turn away.

This day and night are finished.

I turn back the bed.

Now!

Come back into this web.

Circled and invisibled I am. Blacked out into blackness, an ebony exactness, planed and stained jet smooth. Polished and burned; returned beneath this raging squall. The end of it all is nigh, as I lower to you and I. Fingers still interlaced. Heads thrown back, but faced together. I see you clearly, as if never ever everness could ever pull us apart.

Dismounting – I know – exactly where we are. Exactly where we fell when we broke the spell.

I should lift you upon this red sky beast and we should ride away and release the echoes from every canyon, the fields ahead of the stallions, racing on. I should cry at the top of my voice, over the howls that joist and dagger and split, madder than any storm before or since. I should cry, 'Release us!' I would spin and turn us, collect all the pieces and snap each one back into place. I would – if I could! (I would) embrace and elevate you from this coven of lies and deceit. Lose ourselves in the stars we have counted incomplete. Angled and angeled, untangled and cradled in a universe free of layers.

I would that I should, my love, but cannot. Those tiny dots, whirling and unfurling, have been planned into space, precisely positioned, perfectly placed, phased for those fortune's cards. These euphoric charades switch and pitch us, capsize and lift us, pull and push and rush us into this headlong undoing of all the undone.

And now with a kiss and the throw of a dice, a sacrifice that you may remember us – always. Back into life, my love! Back into the breath. I go to Whisperer and stairs and hallways and layers of sheets pulled back from the bed, the web – reddening skies receding. Lantern lit. It swings in and out, shadow and light, irreverent and devout. Waits upon my return; albeit I was never there to have left. This must be done. No regrets. Because all shall restore and the free rivers chase us back into the sea. Can you believe they run free? I cannot see you suffer. But trust me, and remember – you know the other.

I place my lips onto yours.

This is not a kiss goodbye.

This is you and I uniting.

Neither thunder or lightening or any runaway storm.

The skies are filled with our stars.

Sourced from the heavens, written in, because this destiny is ours. Somewhere, lost among the trillions of towers, your other seeks to correct that which is ours.

This is not a kiss goodbye.
This is you and I uniting.

As surely as Yin turns Yang and Yang turns Yin, so we begin and rebegin and spin and begin again. All the circles are closed as the stars go out and relight anew.

Your lips dissolve upon my lips.

Your words scatter and hoop into the loops sealed to the peeling storm behind us. Reveal and wheel. Healing as they reel yet away and away.

Your ruffle and whirr to that temple obscured, screened before the fabric of decaying edges.

Is this what you mean?

As I open my eyes.

Your hand in mine.

Stained with the wine, *chinked*, and saluted to time.

Is this what you mean?

As the world of light floods in and rings that tolling bell.

Is this how it becomes?

Those words slip into another world and spell a spell to divide as each side turns the other and the other turns this.

Is this what you mean?

As I look into your face.

Sweet dreamed foreverness.

Did you make a wish, my love?

As I try to move.

That we might, in our everness, glimpse the truth?

As I allow the air in, damp and rotten, forgotten and lost in a hole below the sun. Its zenith burns in the turns and orbits of that which has us hid here. In the shadows and tumbledown darkness. In the black and heartless of never-to-be-found.

Did you tie into this a knot impossible to untie?

As I pull my arm around and turn on my side.

Is this what you meant, my love?

When you placed your lips on my lips?

You and I uniting?

Lightening, my love.

And thunder, my love.

As we run, like rivers, free into the sea.

The *other* borrows time as if seconds and moments could be shuffled like cards, as if tarot and destined tomorrows could be laced into ours. As if, indeed, freed ghosts might look up as his shadow crosses the moon. Look down and around, for the sky already blooms – the dead have risen and these forevers, these endeavours, have neither beginning, nor end. Imprisoned in these twists that send us, not to the sea, but through the folds rolled back upon themselves.

Entwined and aligned we are.

Divine, yet undefined.

These lines speed straight to the curve.

Was that the wish, my love?

This body struggles to turn.

Hand in hand.

Come!

Are you not meant to have awoken?

Spell broken?

Are we not meant to resume?

Is this not complete now?

Isn't this done?

Woodland and an errand for stars revealing. Jam jars and butterflies, fireflies in the evening. Hoping to kiss you, wistfully mine. Hoping this bewitchment parallel times, overlines and underlines, shatters the fragments fragmented by all those eternities we might have encored together, anchored to a feather released into the cosmic wind. These things. These rings and devotions, perpetual motioned to the metronome exactness of everything after or before the grace of God.

In the absolution of everything.

Every dream dies its death.

Upon the tallest pinnacle of every regret.

Each little piece removed.

Pulled from the snarl.

Conveniently lost, as The One corrects.

And the *other* collects.

And repositions into a snarl of own.

Incomplete we are, my love. Our woodlands and storms and kisses receding, leaving us as the night leaves for morning. Incomplete and drained we are, as the weavers begin reweaving.

Your lips are cold.

Roll you into my arms.

Your breath is as still as a pin-drop chills the silence.

Embraced in this defiance of yours.

Is this it?

How it is meant to be?

You and me, me and you, you and me. Here? Wrapped together as we exchange life for life and life for death. Ashes to ashes. All we have left are our stars spinning between dusk and dawn.

Is this it?

Is this *really* it!

'Ahh!' – Come with me and I will discover a magic in a season hidden away somewhere. Stay with me. I will carry you. There is an incantation, a spell out there, just waiting to be cast – to bring you back. Trust me! I know this to be true. You and Me. Me and You. Nothing more.

H ere she comes!
Bride to meet the groom.

Look how the storm falls behind her!

Look how the spirit inside her kicks out anger and fire. Illuminates all below. Cusps the spires, blazing holes, throwing sparks from horses hooves. Throwing dice as the hounds pursue, chasing to me.

Really!

'Ha! Ha!'

This *was* meant to be.

Another bride!

Come!

You have left *him* behind.

Now you are truly mine.

Join me in this shuffling of destined destinies.

I am already here to meet you – to greet you.

Come!

Climb down into my arms.

You see.

Dressed in white.
Perfect!
I may be darkness.
But remember. (when the time is right)
I become the light.

And shivered and dazzled, crushed and scraggled, the jangled jangles of the iron bell fade. Church bells and hells bells ring-ringing, the rivers that flow to the towers are bringing light into their darkness. The circle sealed and all the clocks have restarted, and the dust that clogged them, and the ghosts that mourned them, departed.

This is the hour into which the universe recorrects and sets every number, sum total, and card; selects and reselects until every quantum of nothing is entered and restarted, rebooted and remastered, resumed and distorted, inverted correctly upside down.

The square root of every crooked mile multiplies and nullifies every back step closer, every roller coaster host to the whisperer in the web.

At last, all is quiet. The storm (torn between the then and the now) finally gone. The horses. Kisses. Churches and trains. Reds and woodland greens and everything lost inbetween – forgotten and of no worth. The threads are as one, as if never stolen or cut from the earth. Here, at last all forgotten, the world of providence settles back into its lazy wilderness called the curse of the eternal wheel.

Step off it, of course, and the seals of Solomon are opened, the universe deep-oceaned as witches and hags pitch black into bags for their potions.

Yet that is all over.

The bride and groom are as one.

The indecipherable clues are none.

C lass dismissed!
　　Patterns shift and collide, swirl and slide, eddy and rearrive. Return with a kiss. Groom lifts the bride. Returned. Side by side.

Remember the dance?

Our horizons?

How they advanced and eclipsed as our sailing ships, real or imagined, slipped effortlessly toward the pale. On the skyline awaiting His bride – this lonely place for souls to divide. And you and I. Beyond all of this and all of that we could neither stack or collapse or shatter so much as a jot of any of this.

But remember the dance?

How our horizons, perchance, liquefied as we moved and ran into the whirls and whorls of nothing at all. How it all disappeared, reappearing only as rhapsodies.

The dance, my love, illusioned. But I swear, I held you in my arms as we stepped apart and we played our farewells. I swear, as we watched the ghosts gathering at the stairwells.

Yet, I have heard your every word, every sigh and

promise to become one. Have listened and trusted and waited in this darkness. Waited and reasoned. I have belated every breath already swathed in death, grotesque, hairpinned, pulled back upon itself. There is a whisper of something, almost lost behind that illusioned, faraway horizon. It swishes and hisses as if waves against another shore.

'Shhh!'

It shingles and rushes, mutters and yet speaks of nothing. Emptiness pushing into a world we do not understand. The void looking in upon itself.

'Shhh!'

And now awake, those waves break very quietly over that faraway shore. Too far away to be sure. If that is where you are. Cannot hear your voice or your sighs, or your gentle assurance that all will be well. The storms and red cloud horses have all blustered away. Through the greys and the veils and the grim, I cannot believe you have left me for Him.

Is this it?

As I slowly awake.

A sweet sacrifice that I may live?

Look away, then. I shall sieve away every grain of sand and speck of dust; and, if I must, pile them at His gates. Nothing ever turned but for want. And nothing ever stopped – only the clocks – unless to haunt the tears and hurried repairs of this ruptured web, one end tied to the bottom of those stairs.

Another fish-hooked into the snares of this world. Unreal world. Gossamer threads are destinies lifting with the vague swell of His breath. Tied in and knotted.

Another hook cut into a horizon remote. Beyond a sea fed by rivers, free running, chopping and churning, with any news from the other side.

Too many hooks and tethers pulled taut across the abstracts of so-called faith and trust. Numberless corners securing one end to another. These hasps that pin and cover smother the emptiness beneath. Beneath the beneath, below the below, asunder the deepest depths. Such places, more or less, allowed to their own abandonment. This is where the universe sleeps dark matter. Slumbers and hibernates. Scattered into a trillion dreams. Spattered, as stars across a canvass.

As a ship sail swells, so too these criss-crossed stairwells, as if vented in a breeze, as a sheet ripples and lifts, lowers and drifts a little, pulling upon the ties, but never letting go.

My eyes are open, my love. My head full of everness. I look at you, my love. Your dress is streaked white earth, and pressed against this stillness.

For what energy remains, I rise upon one arm.

Every mis-read star curves a path to where we are and have arrived. Just as you and I had arced that small leap to here. A flavour of wine. Your hand in mine. Dismissing the promised horses. Crashing slopes over undergrowth, we fell and tumbled, spun and jumbled, stopping where we lie. A small sky framing the windowed world above.

It is a long way down to here. And a long climb up to that high world of light. Here there is only damp and darkness. How this started, just a leap from a train, that we might remain undivided and slip your troublesome ghost.

Now, slowly to knees, pain squeezing between sinew and bone. Drawing in breath. Your face at rest, still dreaming away and alone. I no longer hear your voice, my love; from the other side. That which switched the great divide. Where your troublesome groom awaits.

But, divided we are.

And the storm abates.

Sacrifice!!

Do you truly believe I should count every breath as we counted every star? Do you truly imagine I would choose life?

Not ever!

It is a struggle to rise.

How do I carry you when I cannot even stand?

How do I draw you through, pulling at your hands and ankles, tangled and bruised, completely unable to move you.

Do you truly believe I might sparkle into this existence we call the present? Do you think?

Do you think, for one slight moment, we might yield to any of this? I don't think.

But.

I know.

Regardless of how we could have been fooled. Our souls are ravelled and twisted and paired for all time. The webs may dance upon the breath of the dead below. The threads may tear and repair, every cry of despair is here, all illusions and grand delusions vibrate and tremble and assemble before the *now*.

Not by even a leaf's length have I been able to move

you. Not even the thickness of one blade of this damp, unforgiving, grass.

Heart pounds.

Falling away – as my energy depletes.

As if falling from that train, all over again.

'It is beautiful.'

'Then, take my hand.'

The door is opened.

The world rattles past.

Scarlet horses slashed across the sky.

Just you and I.

Your hand pulls on mine.

Gently.

Fast as every beating heart.

The smallest shadow departs a tower, across the heavens to stand testimony to this destiny's undoing. Every above and below.

He awaits.

'I love you.'

'I love you.'

And we let go.

Ha! Ha!
  Look at him!

Look at him indeed!

Unable to even rise to his knees!

See how he heaves and pulls. And all to no avail.

See how his own weakness breaks him.

I struggle not to laugh. To think he might return you to his world. Return you to life. Man and wife!

Never!

Ha! Ha!

How does he hope to imagine, by this or any other means, he could possibly pull you back to the track of trains? And in that hope gain access to life and death?

Your mortal remains, my dearest, are immoveable, manoeuvrable to none except mould and canker, incurable and damp and stamped this into every broken heart.

Poor thing.

He thinks there is hope.

Yet apart and untogethered he evokes the spell of love. Unforevered, poor thing. Love plays no part in the running of the web, or the runners and wheresoever they go. Such, I say, is upon my own arrangement, engaged upon whims and selfish merriment. Such a thin layer, this sediment that settles over the dust of the damned. Yet here I am. *Here* – Raising my lantern. These great halls of vastness and mantled shadows. My whispers are particular and delicate. Such hushed wherewithalls develop this into purest, unshatterable, illusion.

Poor thing.

He begins now to cover himself with leaves and moss. Cuddling and burying in next to you;

hopes washed into a faraway corner. Or a faraway shore. You can hear the universe breathing as the waves shingle, push and draw the galaxies in, turning and spiralling, blurring and entiring the entireness of eternity within a sacred moment.

I raise this lantern, bride, as you move toward me. Behind you. Around you. Fires of hell blaze and burn.

Will you not watch this with me?

Your lover's concerns are of no matter.

Let us join as Yin and merge as Yang and total the sum and remove the divide that hangs over our ghosts that they may dance awhile. Their candles light and flicker and sway as we engage the beguiled.

I see you clearly, bride and dearest, as you approach through these sombre halls. Your spirit chars the very essence of your arrival. Am I not the totality of despisal? Do you not realise? Reprisals are futile in this world of forever.

What is it you expect?

I should withdraw and ply homage to your innocence?

Or – perchance – deliverance in an undelivered neverness?

Here!

Take my hand.

Our bed awaits.

As the ghosts assemble and peruse their escape.

You had hoped, in a hidden heart, there would be a space, some forbidden place, some hideaway knoll into which we could crawl and draw the undergrowth up over our heads and kick in our heels, the remains of the dead, who lie undisturbed, asleep in their webs.

Hence here we divide. All our sorrows untied. All our breaths and deaths, loves and lies, broken by a dream and moments hesitation.

There is nothing to say and nothing to add; nothing to show or frame or say we ever had. Here lies the moment. Let it rest in peace. We must remain in silence and remember this. Let us cross our hearts and hope to die, let us whisper a prayer and close our eyes. Let us go. Let it go. Let it dissolve away.

This is where all words run out.

Devout.

Weeping at the moon.

This is where it all ends.

This is where we belong.

Finished, tied and tarred the knot.

Gone and gone.

Gone.

The *otherness* transcends, lifts and descends, carries enchantment in both eyes, and a something in its beak as it peaks and lowers and swoops and skewers, fan-tailed and veering free. Visioned and far, locating the hole beneath a star. Sees and curves to arrive, plateau skies dipping and drawing away, with his loop of broken thread. They: overgrown and overgrowthed, embraced and merging as one.

This thread. This run of missing time. Removed by the weavers to correct the lines stretched crosswise to any other. This passage of lives sliced from the ether, measure for measure, predestinies and testimonies untogethered.

Extracted threads.

These are the heartbeat patterns, the days and nights, the years and *everything* that never happened. These are the loves and lives, deprived and *neverbeen*, the falls and the rise of absent inbetweens. They are the dreams undreamt, terms and seasons sent, cut, swirling into the neverness of no account. No amount, or count, of none *ever* added to this. No equations or corrolations formed of anything ever summed to a kiss.

Sobeit.

And so it is done.

Discarded and unrecorded. Dropped. Stopped. Forgotten.

Did not happen.

Did not occur.

Did not stir so much as a leaf.

Twisted preordained lines.

And from that moment until the next, severed and reset; the dice is rethrown and cards turned again. The readings redetermined, reconfigure the web. Weavers busy fingers respinning every braid, altering all the courses, and dismantling the never made.

And so it is.

Exactly as that.

Every conceivable forever merely a provision for that

which is cast. Ordained and guarded. Cut and trimmed. Aligned as per whims befitting to Him. And all that He might take another bride. Another to add to the hall of trillioned candles. Loved and abandoned, the random reprieves the planned; the chance and background rhythm that urges every soul to dance. That is He – The spoiler of perfect order, the flaw and *dis*order of all the countless infinities. Possibilities. Captured in an equation and shattering the spell of creation.

For such as it is, and for all that ever mattered, the shatters are reflected, slithered and exacted, sharp as needles stabbing into the skies as steeples. From henceforth all generations shall call thee blessed. The choirs are ringing as rook wings his spiral descent. In this event, that thread cut from the loom, here is the shadow that crosses the moon.

And not a moment too late.

July to August rising.

Beneath, below, above and on.

And on.

Mesmerising.

But do not look!

Rook lifts and drops. Drifts and hops between this world and that. And, exactly, on and betwixt this and every dream, every single moment, every solitary micro-cosmic never-has-been or ever will be again.

Until now?

Perhaps.

And down.

Deeper down to go.

Down.

Down.

Down.

Deeper and deeper.

Between the veils.

Into the pale.

For here is the truth.

In the Allness of All and all before. There are doors and there are windows. The prophecies stall and stop. The clocks address the chorus, raised voices epoched, but lost – like children, in fact – within faraway woods. That they should tarry awhile, and that they would, were not the stormbringer already colouring the sky. Were not that chorus announcing all of this.

Windows and doors. Worlds to explore. Hideaway knolls and holes behind stars. On-hundred-and-fifty-six in all!

Still down and down.

Deeper down to go.

Skim-gliding between planes, dimensions renamed Strangeness and Charm, Up and Down and every configuration of every constellation that turned in the heavens.

Stealthy and silent, this pilot thin-edges the alignment just as a knife slides into flesh. Each pressed, neither more nor less, neither for or against, but to itself every world be true. And in each of these worlds, he builds towers, too.

C ome!
   Lay upon my bed.
Sweet bride.
Sweet sighs.
Roll like thunder across your heart.
Come!
Lay here, up so close.
Your forgotten world evokes nothing and nothing undermines or redefines *anything*.
And – if *anything* – we are as Yin and Yang combined.
Only *now* – darkness and light.
And now – we might unite as two.
And now – forget him.
There is only *Me*.
And there is only *You*.

no.

H ere!
   Let me slide my hand over your breast. Naked and sweet and caressing thee with an enlightened kiss.
Here!
Let me pull you unto myself.
Feel the hardness between your thighs.
This is You and I.
Do you understand?
Closer!

Let me feel your body surrender.
Let me feel.
And let me enter.
Pushing and forcing.
Yin into Yang.
You need to understand!

no.

If I were, for a moment, to pause and untwist all of this, there would be nothing. If I were so much as to blink, *chink* a toast to the neverendment of the eternal wheel, I would celebrate, a sip to every facet of every defracted, flickering appeal. Never so much as idle occasion, somewhere lost in the realms of these hallucinations. Tarry and haunt, they do. Such euphoria! This phantasmagoria of begotten, forgotten souls, stirred, disturbed, like mud bottomed pools into a maelstrom of ditherings, fuelled – exactly – by nothing itself.

Yet, between umber and amber, they waltz as one. Between slumber and samba they each belong to rhythm in the midst of some beyond. Every movement illussioned in the vast hallways of Om. Gone to none. Gone to dust. Gone to dishevelled decay.

And so the dancers are hurried away.

And in the attics and cellars the spirits decant, essences and effervescences, bubbles bubbling into this masquerade of cause and effect. These vague prisms deflect, but are unable to hide.

It is time to decide.

Allow the bride her due.

Every default and summersault tightroped across the ether.

Is it time to stand back?

Or is there an exactness in this disorientation of *now*?

no

B ut it is already too late. Checkmate!

except for one.

F ear not to tread, sweet angel, in these shadows, in these valleys, in this darkness. Fear not for want of vision, or need to believe. Mark this moment; for *I* see him, too. The *other* as another turning tide. Cycles and rotations. Revolutions and revelations. Slide free between the worlds that separate you and I. Inbetween the curls and curtains that shift, yet abide, according to schemes based upon nought.

Tao coils itself, perpetuates, figure-eights, and steps out of this ill-fated parade. Candy-striped, this darkness and light, hoops and stacks, circles exact. This voyager strobes and slants, *his* towers calling, but falling behind. This journey incorrectly signed, designed to mislead and lose. Yet those, as these, blow and breeze, like ships fully sailed, like the rips, fish-tails, splits and frills tweezed and re-repaired – teezed – and pulled away. Tiniest threads from the omnipotent web. Tiny-tiniest shreds misdirecting to hidden worlds.

However, our rook flies straight and true. Between diversion and lies and disguises set to mislead from here.

Lands upon a corner overlooking strange order. Complex weaves stretching as far as any eye can see. Hooked into the cracks that divide the worlds. Tightened and pulled to ensure every fold turns as per the One's great will. And somewhere beyond line of sight, creation centres itself, divides darkness and light. And somewhere deep below, vast hallways run phantoms through the flickers of a lantern swinging. And a little way off; across to the side, a handful of brides patiently check the threads; running the silk between their fingers. Silk wound in silk, turned and wound and rewound until as thick as cable. Entwined, wrapped and primed, taut and black as sable. Silk – but not silk. Such stuff, soul stuff, that dictates every soul's place and His whims in this grand scheme of things.

At the centre of all this. This. This magnificent adjustment of *everything*, He presides. This epicentre, this hub by which every atom communicates with every other, oversees, but does not see.

Our rook remains here. Thread in beak. Curious eyes lit by curious brides crossing slowly toward him. This free spirit, free-willed, never written in or out, and only now upon an errand of own.

Ever slowly to cross, whispering on their way.

Rook patiently waits.

Patiently watching as the flux and flex of every destiny connects: wrapped – every single one around every single other.

Watching. As the skit-scattering fortunes slither away. All those predestinations play out their hands.

Watching each dice; first, twice, thrice and more, fail to land so much as a double and one free go to the score. Double-six. Double-nothing.

Watching these hexagonal splices, honeycombed slices, cross-running, diverging, converging, uniting – but always, almost, fingertip touching. Every breath and *every* breath breathing in and out as one.

But, alas, time has come.

The brides arrive and gather around.

'How is it you can be free if we are not?' our rook is addressed.

'How is it?'

'How is it you are not in there?' (she points down into the web)

'You are not written in.'

'How is it?'

'Why is it you wait here?'

'Why that thread in your beak?'

'I believe he is unable to speak!'

'I believe that thread was once removed and off-centred.'

'What is it, then?'

'Is it a love story?'

'And what are you doing with it?'

Our rook steps from side to side.

'Tis a tale of love, indeed!'

Side to side.

'Why would it be removed? Why would it be denied?'

'Let us see.'

'Where does it belong?'

Released into their fingers.

'Are we able to right a wrong?'

Side to side.

'And what of the Divine Will?'

Look to one another.

Little whispers and giggles spill one into the other.

A little look.

A little smile.

And, in a while.

'.....We know where it goes.'

*O*h, great Divine will!
Your flickering lantern swings and splutters, spits and stutters as a fluttering heartbeat about to die. The phantoms murmur, restless, because there are rumours concerning the resistant bride.

This is all that remains.

This is all there is.

Did you not hear the click in the crack as I returned a kiss? Did you not see the seam in the black, a fault that fate had missed? Did you not feel the defect splitting? Separating random from fixed? All this – because your new bride will not comply.

I despise you.

Such folly.

Your portals between worlds slide hopelessly away. Because the threads in Your web are already relayed. Because the twists in the braids turn back upon themselves. Because Your heavens and hells are muddled and jumbled. Your sums and fortunes all tumbled and broken. Death – by any other token.

This bed You lay before me, white sheets turned back. Crisp and alluring, fooling other brides, perhaps. Time-lapsed and delicate, slow-motioning and exact. What would you have me do? Come running? What would you possibly expect? That I might abandon my one, true, love and defect into this delusion of yours?

What would you do?
Your bed awaits. Sanctioned.
No ordinary church.
I may lay upon it.
But I forbid You to touch.

Nonesense.
Such quaint ramblings.
I respect your innocence and sweet reverie.
But this is not how it is meant to be.
You must listen.
Yes!
Lay upon My bed.
Your body perfect.
Do not be scared.
Lay back and tremor.
Cast a net over your dreams.

You are correct.

But not everything is as it seems.

All those worlds. *Every* world. Every one is balanced and imbalanced, one beside the other. Deliberately unified, tied and tethered to every other across every divide. Togethered and whenevered to every bride's arrival.

For such as it is, counted in and counted out, the eternal wheel revolves, greets one in and allows another one out. And around and around and around it whirls. Every life is a dance, balanced between every trillioned world. Every soul. *Every* soul numbered and accounted, amounted and summed – zero divided by one.

Not everything is as it seems.

You are permitted to dance – within the frame.

You are permitted to choose, but not to change.

Lay back and relax and let it all go.

Such is the way. There is nothing more to know.

Lay back and allow these energies engage, this metamorphosis embraces, the spirits replace and dance and sail as ships to their own horizons. Breathe it all in and breathe it all out. Let your chest rise and fall and erase your doubts.

I will lay beside you and promise not to touch.

Only to watch.

As I lie down.

What do you expect to find that nobody else has found?

Do not turn away.

I ask you once again.

What – that nobody else could find?

I turn.

This bed is soft and would wither me into the embryonic sleep of perpetual motion if I were only to close my eyes. It would devour me and return me to the axis heart, a kick to restart and, allow me to slide back to beginning again. Redeem and renew, rejoin the queue and release next bride in waiting.

Very soft and enchanting.

But will not consent or sanction – any of this.

This egg-timer sand. This so very slight-of-hand. This trickery and charm. It has all gone wrong. The undoing is done.

Look away.

This day, this now, *this irreversible plough turns out lines of its own in a field below Your web. Your corners unhitched, unpicked and liable to collapse. Your whimsical merriment entraps You. Other randomness overlaps You – but You have not seen* it *yet.*

Soft as feathers melting into dreams.

Drowsy, dozey, faraway teams of horses stormy red. Woodlands spread, two children stepping in and out of circles, out and in and out inverted, invisibled and reverted. Undone. Returned.

'Was that a kiss?'

Your eyes swallow this.

'Invisible?' you said.

At some point to turn and return your kiss..

At some point to run, run-running out-of-circle-kissed; a storm upon our heels.

See how we run!

How the clouds congeal and take shape.

How they peal and bellow and break above our heads. Every red as could ever ignite, exit day and entrance night. Every maroon and scarlet, garnet and magenta. Every sienna burnt and rose off-centred. Every flush cut-throat, oxidized and brushstroked across these skies. All we see are horses and nowhere to hide.

Softly feathers.

Falling away.

Deeper and deeper.

See how we play.

Fingers into filigree, black and wrought symmetry. Bedframe head all furls and twirls, latticed and furled in sleepy fingers. Cold as ice as touch writes its way along little twists and sweepy curls, loops and spirals, skeletal angles tangled among these – and among these – the outline of a key.

'We know where it goes.'

Our rook lifts upon her shoulder. Looks from one eye into the other.

'We are not dead, you know.'

'Nor are we alive,' says another.

'Somewhere inbetween, I guess.'

'Somewhere else. Undiscovered.'

The thread she has taken no longer than a kiss, but shorter than an embrace. She has it wound carefully around her wrist and walks with elegant grace. She admires the weaves and strands, interwoven braids and detailed yarns, and a structure unto itself. A micro structure configurated and assimilated according to its weaver and every believer that ever turned a key in an unknown door. This is for sure. As this is for that. *That* and *this* are opposites to eternal laws.

But here – undiscovered – the small in the finite, this bride pauses at a junction in the web and lightly floats across the tightropes that design heavens and redefine hells.

The other brides follow, giggling amongst themselves.

Very gently she undoes the thread surround.

To where this loop once belonged.

A sigh to lock it back into place.

In an instant, time divides.

Done and undone.

Undoing, respun, respinning, replaced.

Throwing stars in disarray.

Constellations cascade and cloak.

Undoing all the horoscopes.

'I shall take this key.'

All the majorettes, usherettes, and percussionists march to their own advance. One-two. Two-two. See the parade entrance. Devoured and deflowered and sweet as every numeric – one-two, two-two, effervescent and psychedelic. Such the beat of the armied souls, striding but never arriving. Crushed and bluffed beneath horizoned millstones that grind this seed, blows like tumbleweed, lost brides to slopes and slides. And – in the twinkling of an eye – just a background noise that fades in receding tempo.

'Not guilty!' their drums rattle, picking their pace.

One-two.

Two-two.

Deciphering the morse-code phrase.

Synchronised above and below.

Here is the point of letting go.

Hitherto, we dress and anoint.

As we approach the jumping off point.

And the beat continues to fade and jade in this palette of blacks and greys. And the lures and hooks baited to seduce via sweeping circles, weighted in our circus of broken days.

'Not guilty!' they clatter and narrate.

Before it is too late.

'Not guilty!'

All souls deployed as they step into the void.

'You just kissed me back!'

'I know. Quickly! We don't have long!'

'What happened? It has all turned back!'

'We have an ally.'

'I remember a train.'

'And we have a key!'
'But we must hurry.'
'These are our woods.'
'What happened?'
'You were watching. You saw it, too.'
'Kiss me.'
Lips-to-lips.
Arms around.
Wrapped tightly.
Everything as it was.
As it was meant to be.
'But – look – key!'
'What are we looking for?'
'A lock!'
'Come.'
And we're running.
'Where are we going?'
Skies are reddening again!'
'Come!'

H ere we go!
There is a tree.

Because the centre of forever is wherever it needs to be. Branches stretched, pulling at the heavens, roots twisting down deep into the dense nightmares of trickery and fraud and rift and unrest, reaching out, across, into north, into south, east and west. Pulling at time, addressing sublime, furthermore council between dark and divine. Wide boughs arrive, meridian and parameter, circumference and diameter, tendrils folding around every heart – beating or not. Start and stop, aligning the clocks; sweet perambulators of time, wound up and wound around, winding in and rolling down to cycle and sequence.

Every leaf counting every soul.

Every caress.

Every afterall.

Sunset and rise.

Every pulse crystalised.

Synchronised.

One.

A nest within that tree, up amid the highest spray; overlooking, undershooting, fashioned into braids. A crown, perhaps? Or wreath? Depending if above or beneath. Or refuge, if somewhere lost inbetween.

For the moment this position is empty, the owner away on errand. The errant breeze and inherent leaves ruffle and rustle and flutter concerned; impatiently awaiting successful return.

Arbiter and observer to such undoings documented in the gnarled bark scrawls. Details recalled on account to bear witness. Furrowed and scripted and carefully submitted, this submission underwritten by All.

And all for all as always call forth upon those free souls, to whisper oaths to all of those who stand testament of turning time. However, they between themselves keep secrets, like butterflies in jars. This mediator between heaven and hell impartial to effect or cause. Hence, it may seem prudent to all concerned, conciliation be suspended and temporarily adjourned.

Rewebbed, repaired and turned again. Turned, returned and back again. All recorded and all prepared, addressing on owner's return. But, so far, the enterprise and undertaking has moved the stars and upturned the moon. Hereby sentenced – doomed to death. Hereby hushed in shallow breaths. Hereby unlocked unlockable chains, fixed, unfixed, and thereby changed.

Forever?

A trillion, trillion, trillion souls shuffle forward from hole to hole. The lantern swings, but hallways empty; the gates of everness hint at entry. Yet, our displaced host slips dimension, rips, slits at these corrections. See Him manoeuvre, disorientated. See Him searching for His bride, shuffling worlds like cards, like tides lost from shore. See Him demand, command a restore and return of His bride to be.

Destiny?

You see?

But, this tree stands tall, despite all. Its long limbs spread, elongated, immense bole braced and serrated against a jagged backdrop of rumoured spoil – when, in fact, there is nothing at all – bar towers and an occasional sky.

Underlit, underbelly fire. Scaled dragons attired. Assembled to replace red horses as twilight hurries on. Such crimson – infused into *everything*. Such an offering. Not horses – but beasts fuelled by flame, ablaze, burning out the horizon.

As such was meant to be.

For hearts and circles.

Invisible and free.

Below.

This.

Tree.

There is a door.

Only children can see.

Hidden, veiled, concealed.

Even if they had a key.

'*W*e must first look for our circles!'

(but these are hidden away)

All I can see are trees. We are lost as we are delayed.

'*Stop! Try to remember. Try not to break the fall between then and now. Remember how it changed with a kiss?*'

I do.

'Give me your lips.'

'*Was that a kiss?*'

Galaxies repair and wheel ageless and surreal. Positron and electron collide. Dark matter and anti-matter allied and rearranged connected, even light years apart; promising a spark that will destroy *everything*, one day.

'*Keep looking!*'

Earth and weed and woodland floor.

'*Cannot be far from here.*'

July dust, no more.

'*Try to remember.*'

A taste upon lips.

'*Here!*'

Pursed as her finger points and she swings her hips.

'*Look!*'

And a circle drawn into soil. 'Kiss me back.'

And she does.

Then, climb inside together.

Did that really happen?

Where are we now?

And now – forever.

White dress cropped, stopped above the knee. Hair curled, unfurled. One hand opened. In the other: something taken from He.

'*Kiss me again.*'

Here am I!
I turn the cards and roll the dice. I decide! I decide!

Here am I!

I choose and select My every bride (because it amuses me to do so).

Throw the dice. Random choice, yet structure within disorder. Thread the stars. Turn the cards – some with fingernailed corners.

Ha!

Random Me! Random Me! Provided I am allowed to choose. I charge a fee, if you need to see, an occasional win, but mostly lose.

Yet – What is this! Who is this – Playing me at my game? I control all fortune, twisted to suite My means. I choose and allow some to my bed. All is knotted and lined into the web.

Who is this? Tampering with time? Who has undone and redone that which is rightfully mine?

That, once again, I should override another, ensuring this bride becomes My lover?

How is it the sky reddens, just as it did before? Only, this time dragons, not horses, paused and corrected and restored. And now you have your key. We know of this superseded destiny. An overlooked thread snagged loose from the web, allowed us a kiss, yet forwarded time; but I remember all this. I remember a church, and a train, and you; the journey; you were still in white, man and wife.

I love you with all my life.

Wife-to-be (it seems).

All my life.

Still, here we are, one-hundred-and-fifty-six stars, and counting.

What have we become?

And what of you and me?

Again – Where are we?

Trapped, perhaps, in this prismed framework, overlocked, half-stopped, unsure of direction. Enticed inside, trapped butterflies all flutter and flapping, capped jar tapping out rhythms of escape. Is it not too late to release? Or already too damaged to fly?

You and I.

Hypnotised by the swimming sun in this childhood woodland-cum-place-of-return.

But your eyes still smile and melt into mine when our lips touch, hips touch, and we dissolve into one. For children, indeed, where magic weaves spells and charms and storms seem to gather quickly around us.

Dragonfire, this time; on this decaying cycle slow-strobing toward world's end. Burning, unfurling inferno delayed. There will be no horses, not now we have this mend – permanent or not.

But there may be a storm. We can watch it pass by. And when it has cleared and steered away and died we shall sit beneath the stars.....still counting.

However.

I see how the beasts unfold their wings, encompassing – everything – dark reddening, dried blood entering the moon which has become a heart and arteries inflate into plumes, clouds pulled apart. And the rumble of their breaths in firey chests angrily boil as the coil of their tails push long snouts into a terrorised sky.

O ur rook watches the storm with interest. Steps from side to side. Looks from bride to bride, as they float and drift and shift as weavers across the web. Effortlessly tying the maelstrom in.

'They need a storm,' says one.

'It's where they belong,' nods another.

'Should I be tying one in? Romantic, don't you think?'

Rook watches on.

'Isn't it time you moved on?'

'Don't you have things to collect?'

'Towers to build?'

Side to side. Thinking, perhaps. Considering the dragons.

S trange energies wrap and snake, shape, form, coil and break. Surge, assemble, a structured advance these demons and/or angels dance outside the gates of hell; because heaven is too far to climb, and the gods, these days, rarely assign to disorder.

Strange developments enveloping these vast and lofty skies; but nowhere to hide. Those snouts flare out and singe and ember, receding as evening hurries on. Pyre upon pyre, monstrous choirs lifting, rising and shifting, purifying the air.

Strange powers these custodians, these guardians behind, behind and behind. Strangely strange these stains on this eve. For behind the wheels crushed by the wagons the driver slides fire ahead of his dragons. Unwilling to give quarter, rarely assigned to such disorder. His scout on errand and post vacated, tampering time and lines and distorted designs, upside down and inside out; converse, reversed and each collide, all universes tip contrariwise.

Hence the battlecry preceding first, second and final stand and the locking and relocking of Yin into Yang. Hence these beasts demonstrating strength and honour, roused and raised, if, by that final hour, armies might muster and rally for war.

*T*his is where I heard the whisperer first.
            Warned me of the storm.

A different storm than this.

The first storm.

Remember?

But, before that, he spoke of this tree.

Peculiar properties.

Almost without words.

As if signing behind a door, slightly ajar, demanding to be closed. As if a ghost might slip through.

Though, I am not so sure whether that would be in, or out. Here.

Returned to where we were.

But it is not the same.

See how the horses – not horses anymore – great beasts stretch across the heavens, cleansing the sky before the storm rolls in.

It had been the horses. Prepared to collect me. The storm needed to power them through. So He said.

But not these. Not dragons! If that is what they are. Made of cloud. Nothing more. Except for ghosts and spirits and brides to ride. Side by side with the devil.

The quick and the dead.

Turn back the bed.'

*A*nd thus rook has lifted high above the weavers, up, over the web; enlightened believers; brides unwed. Continuing their day, lightening the shadowed doorways and hallways, unfixing all the refixed threads.

Ascending, he oversees, wings spread, engaging the warm thermals that rise from the world far below, to confront a storm welding earth, air, fire and water, mixing new and old. An alchemist muddling elements as though hidden in every fold there might be a something to remedy all of this. This. Which began with a touch of lips. And the dragons bring news, because the clocks muse as the semi-conscious awake. Make no mistake, this report, from the start, imparts no solution, other than confusion. Make no error or misjudgement, the fulfilment and annulment of marriage burns in a fire ahead of the beasts. The deceased are not dead at all; and, indeed, never were. But awakening now as Whisperer vows vapour and rouse the trillions from their sleep.

Higher and higher he drifts. Over the cliffs overhanging every ledge, overspanning all the trickeries tangled into the web.

Purpose because of purpose; this free spirit drifts over the rivers heading for the sea, over mists into wrap around breezes shifting, circled and centred. A tree – applecore to all universes, rendered but unseen. He soars between the towers, pillars of everything the world forgot. Stacked to high heaven and racked tall as the sun, each one mirrored by the next, and the next, on and on. And on and ever and ever, over and on his journey above all of this – ensuring nothing has been missed.

This is it! The collection of every deed. In no particular order. Randomly placed one upon the other. Snapped together and locked like lovers. Each moment, every glance. Every word, perchance, poised within a breath, but never delivered. Every unborn romance, every sliver of every mislaid dream, forevered away. Those little melodies only children sing; harmonised hymns, whispered and delayed. A choral invitation awaiting liberation – for those who took the time to pray.

Tower between tower.

Beast upon beast.

Bringing the rains.

Burning away any revelation heralding the end of the world.

'*I*t's beginning to rain.'

    'How quickly the sky darkens.'

(slow percussion on leaves)

'*Here, safe in this circle, as we left it – invisible – just you and me – secretly.*'

'We cannot hide here forever. I would rather face the storm.'

'He *searches. Cheated from His bride. Cannot find us here, invisibled - even from He. You see, other forces are at work. We just need to believe.*'

'In each other.'

'*Always!*'

'And what of that?'

'*What?*'

'That in your hand.'

'*It's a key.*'

'I see that.'

'*All part of this dance bizarre and our ships to faraway shores. All part of this faulty sequence, oblique, peg-slanted, streaked and smudged, we are. Rubbed, half-erased and sneaked, we are – in and out of this invisibility. What would you have us do?*'

'See how the dragons refuse to fade. It is still not too late.'

'For what?'

'To escape all of this.'

'I love you with all my heart. I will never *let you go. We are as those ships upon which we would dance. We are as far as those vague horizons toward which we advance. And yet our sails fill full as our wind prevails and we let go and untether the dock, for what? Eternity.....?'*

'Love you with all my heart. We are as we are, and – in these rains, unexplained, because that is what we are. I cannot, not for one moment, expect this passing to survive one second more before door and key connect.

'The one this key fits .We must never forget.'

'Do not let this circle become our prison.'

'Shh! Listen!'

'Only rumbles of thunder. No. Here He comes! Rising within the tree!'

'Look for the door.'

'Of course.'

The dragon dance in a now sterile sky configurates contorted, picasso distorted, opaquely applied, razored dust of the dead, a fluorescent roller-coaster for all to see.

'He will come through a door, somewhere there,' pointing.

Yet the ballooning heavens open, as though curtains across a resonating stage. Lowering light embers in a hearth fuelled from burning pages and scripts and words of little consequence. Crackles and snaps and snips that pop spit, split and collide – snaggles and ties (you and I). This theatre awaits groom and bride. Waits and awaits.

'I can hear! The other side of the door.'

This display, from which vision pulls, belongs to the gods and an audience risen from the vaults and hopeless half-lit hallways. This tree, towards which eyes are pulled, guesses at something other than the spells spoken, and a door about to open.

This door undone, unlocked from within, key required, only outside in. I can smell you from here. Taste you in the air. You have my key. Stolen! Ha! I suppose you should know – there is nowhere to go. Destiny prevails, and she dances for me. She is your sister, my first bride, too, don't you see?

Come back.

We shall call this – what? – unwritten and invisible – if that is where you wish to be. But, let Me politely remind you of your sister bride – sweet as she is – reforming and deforming those that stand against her; according to the threads that run through her web. Will undo and change – anything – If that be our whim. I take it all in and count these sins as I would thorns beneath a rose.

So. Where are you now? Where did you go? Back to *him* other, of course. You use magic to hide, but I can feel you here. Close. Invisibled. Who told you this? Not *He*. No. Not *Him*! Dead! Deader than the deadest nothing of nothings of *ever*. Undone and unformed this *creator* of *never* become absolutely *nothing* at all.

Ha! Ha!

There you go!

Just a little sigh.

Something to tell Me you are close by.

Because I know you are here.

With *him*!

Keep the key! It matters nothing at all.

(nothing plus nothing completes)

(two zeros enforced to source the beginnings of life without end)

(Amen)

There you go! Just as you're about to begin, rebegin, or whatever. Reveal yourself; oh, so cleverly hidden. So secretly and completely overridden by this nonsensical nothing at all.

Come!

Back to My bed.

There is still a sentiment tarrying here; because, of course, we are, in the eyes of deadest nullity, eternally wed!

I listen for that sigh.

Come on! Speak to Me!

This is your Husband.

Never mind Destiny! She is My oldest bride – and you can become so much more than all of this. You think a kiss changed *this*?

Well, yes it did.

It did!

It did.

However, kisses and sighs.

Husbands and brides.

This is not precisely love.

This is the supreme emptiness complete and unbroken; perfection of everything unimagined.

It is true.

Key – or no key.

Do your worst. Do what you can do.

Enjoy your life with *him*, without Me. It is your decision. Except – I may need to invite my former bride to override your vision of what is and what will never be.

You and Me.

Meant to be.

According to that sweet bride sister.

Oh! Come on!

Reveal yourself!

That I might, infact, find this destiny and revive the world so utterly tied into nothing of whatsoever. Do you understand? This will upper-hand all the forevers and whenevers *we* know could *never* show a displaced hand.

Turn a card.

I dare you!

This is it.

Show yourself.

Now!

This is it.

Now or never!

Why is the sky full of dragons?!

From side to side.
	A tilt of the head.
In the twinkling of an eye.
Everything as yet.
Every root.
Every faraway star.
Everything yet possible to believe in.
Every – Every.
Every jet that jettisoned and roared into deep space.
Every pillar erected.
To support every dream.
Crumble, falter and regress as the everness of everything subsides.
Our rook divides.
Side to side.
Twinkling eye.
Tilting head.
Describing.
Treetop down.
Wings resounding as a hush upon the bough.
Hints.
Blinks.
Decides.
Splutter-flutter, photons collide, waves subside, particles dance and terminate. Universe assembles in the wake and space of every lucid dream.
The watcher watches this riptide rush, phased between those and these, unable to be crushed, erased, or seized.
The towers jab into their jagged sky. The caverns echo, rattle and die, tombs buried deeper than treasure

or trove, hidden below the foundations of those and these and every column that ever agreed to spike these, as I say, most jagged skies.

Memories forgotten, yet collected, as, indeed, they must.

Abandoned thoughts.

Such is all they are.

Yet.....

Rook pivots.

Surveys.

Contemplates.

Dragons fail to dissipate.

The show is about to begin.

'Roll up! Roll up!'

And down.

Piloting these hallowed hallways. Gathering these souls. No tolls this day as they are steered and urged to gather pace. As they are urged in their temporary trillioned escape, surface to await the Grand Orator, Divine Creator, and the supreme moment of *Now*.

Here! The every evidence of exploit, misdeed and thought, accumulated, preserved and hoarded for such a definition of account. Every tower, top to base, full to overflowing. Every amount of every valuable sum, witness and exhibit from which nothing has become. Hoeing back the random from tiniest seedling shoots. Sowing nought. Poisoning the roots. For want of a particular bride. No soul dies or allows another through. Each queues their turn were a jury to adjourn and debate the correction of a kiss.

Show to begin.

Take a pew.

Sing hallelujah!
Calling the first witness!

Major to minor.
Metaphysical to invisible.

A peculiar interval partakes silent roar – opening of a door – and the emergence of He (first groom to destiny) (first witness accused).

'*There He is.*'

'Shh!'

'*See how He searches, but cannot find us. Not within this circle. See how His nostrils inflate, can smell us in the air. Reversal, but cannot find us here or locate us there. Invisibled, we are. See the door? Across there! Beneath that third bough – the lock, just over to the left.*'

'I see it.'

'*Then, make a wish. And seal it with a kiss.*'

This is it! Now or never!
It is not too late to dance.

***They* are already gathering. Advancing as I seek thee. Interfering crow! What does he – what *do they* know? What do *they* want? Need something better to do. This he and you and never not Me! Never be allowed! You will never be free so long as I draw eternal breath. No death, no more, no less – *always* mine.**

Oblivion to nothing - *Creator*... I make My stand!

'Call that a kiss?'

'Indeed. *And* invisibled.'

'He has gone. Back, through the door. Give Him a little while, and kiss me some more. A little while to lose Himself. A kiss.....'

.....Floor opens.

'Kiss me some more.'

.....Opens – bluebelled and snowdropped, aquamarines and ultrablue, everything before and hereafter. Everything cast to her holy wind and shallow tide, crest subsides, dips and syrups in this eclipsed bouquet, expands and embraces the disarrayed faces of every day remote and essenced into this vast ocean of folding stars.

Lost to the sway of inevitable delays, yet run away and run across, ashes to ashes and dust to dust. Delays by dust, dust to fall, and dust to resurrect.

The ships are set and sails are raised; the null lines unhooked and the anchors weighed. The horizons are measured one against the other, distances deliberated, angled and re-debated, rudder reset and ascend the rigging. The dancers prepare – the show about to begin, kingdoms of heaven and hell and all that lies inbetween. The weavers stilled, the prophets and prophesies unuttered.

Finally.

All is in place and displaced.

Finally.

This kiss embrace and curtains up.

'You are beautiful.'

Then, take my hand.

A udience fully gathered.

Dragons assembled and securing every gate.

Towers presented.

Our rook waits upon a word.

Finally.

From nothing and zero, soft as a sigh, as a butterfly it comes;

'Explain to me how it is the eternal wheel falters. Explain me alterations set to reverse, stopped and restarted this universe. Explain to me.'

Thunder that? Belly of hurricane? Ultimate Leveller? Supreme Deliverer of Justice, was that?

Softest.

Deafening collisions.

Depending upon how one listens.

Woken from sleep?

Angels peep between the drapes behind his throne.

Our rook has flown, leaving the thermals; ever-decreasing circles, lowering through space and time, slants a line of focus whereupon all may gaze.

Here are the hunted, transcending the maze of the web.

Somewhere far below, Hunter, Whisperer, seeks to bed His bride.

Unwilling to partake, see how she hides!

Look a little closer – how He hurries jealously to His first bride, Destiny; a request that she reweave time for His own desires.

But, His unwilling bride has another.

They kissed.

And, hence, because a kiss reveals them as lovers not written in the web, because random and chance ebb and return, so Whisperer has run as quickly as could. Had the weavers zig-zag to steal them from this wood of childhood and dreams. Thrown, then, into the twists and turns that brought them to a church; older, bridging everything that might have been. Wedding bells and beguiling spells that might have seemed anything except their worth.

Look a little closer.

See where we are now.

Entering through a door He has revealed in the tree.

This unwilling bride, though, key in hand, brings with her her lover. They are now as they were meant to be – but, not by fate, nor first bride. This was never embroidered or woven or belonging to either great divide. Random and unchecked.

Look a little closer.

As they open up that door.

'*H*ere we are!'
'It is extremely dark.'
'*Spiral stairs going up.*'

'Spiral stairs going down.'

'*Take my hand.*'

'Down?'

'*Of course, my love. To rescue those souls bound to the waiting gate, where forever belongs to never-ever and every last never could never, ever, ever complete this journey or wait upon a further turn.*'

And yet – corkscrew and helix, as to descend, each one step nearer, as *another* clears.

'As a shadow crosses the moon?'

'*Yes. And flickers between the stars.*'

'One-hundred- and-fifty-six.'

'*See how the web climbs up through the stairs. Imbedded in the walls through the heart of this tree. See how, unbroken, they snake upward and down, heaven-to-hell and to heaven again. See how they form and deform and loop and reform; how they have become the body of this tree. Look how they climb, descend between themselves; how they foretell and parallel and axle at every pitch. Here, the omniverse channels without detour or distortion. Yet here, devotion cautions to continue. This tree uniting heaven and hell together, balanced betwixt all those evers, nevers; and, perhaps, could be again.*'

'Love you with all my heart.'

'*Not a single atom to part or separate.*'

'Not one!'

'*Need to free these souls; a token of our love. As they belong to be free. As per you. As per me.*'

'Stair descending? How do we do this? This bottomless grave. By what means or magic could we liberate or turn so much as a stone?'

'*We are almost there. Feel the stifling damp clinging to every breath we breathe. It layers the lungs, clammy and grotesque and brewed with death and hopeless decay. Sense how, as we submerge, urgency of defiance prevails, eroded into the air. Listen into this dripping darkness as we enter into hollowed rock – even the drips drop silently – stifled dread oversees. Not even an echo as we lower.'*

Without so much as a dungeoned muffle to trouble this lack of oxygen, spiralled descent continues. All sounds and scuffles obliterated long ago. All screams and howls strangulated and drowned as progress downward urges.

Yet high, high above, creator and jury attend to past and present, and a church of somewhere inbetween. Scene rewinding, towers dividing sessions of deemed not now/ever. Our rook outlines and defines every recorded and hoarded activity. For such the way, collected and saved, Whisperer's imbalances have abridged every tincture of time.

Finally, arriving at an archway designing a hunch above a door. Nameplate inscribed, 'Beyond Here Lies The Realm Of Nothing At All.'

As the message suggests, the zeros align for addition. The innumerable souls afford life-in-lieu, pay their toll of silence, and listen, though there is nothing at all. No thing, as ever, could ever have rolled a dice, or turned an expired card. This is where, despite descent, there is nowhere between here and the dim charades of enlightenment.

At last!

Roll up! Roll up!

Show begins.

S ide to side.
　　Bearing witness.

Grooms and brides.

Submit this as testimony to every inaccuracy the distracted see as truth. Present this as a revelation to every affirmation, but herein lies the proof.

Curtain up.

'See how the weavers work quickly to undo the undone. See how these maidens turn and twist the threads, tying and retying all the shortcuts back to origin. Look! How efficient and orderly they restore, repairing to where every line began; currently hooked into the ether; watch, as every other destiny corrects her prescripted cards.

And now I bid, whilst you bear testimony to this. Survey my assembled towers, how high they have grown, how compressed, yet streamlined they have become. Endless to endless horizons, uncounted; each one compacted with extracted collected threads. And collected, in deed, they are. Every single shred of accumulated hoard, a reservoir of all that might have been. Memorabilia and paraphernalia of nothing or ever more. Here, all the everything, every thought, real or imagined. Here – safeguarded and stored.

And now unable to recall or claim return, the maidens hasten, aware, as our waiting audience watches on. Aware the reincarnated participate and dissipate and turn and are gone. Aware, the lantern He brings swings to the rhythm – random is king, and surety knows nothing at all.

Now, as past and present restore, illusions pour

seconds into minutes and hours into days; suggesting time; implying time – when, in fact, there was never time at all. Not a single footstep to fall one ahead of the other. Not a dice was thrown from one moment to the next. Not so much as an amoeba could advance half a molecule from rest.

I say this; our universe is lost in a raindrop hanging in a void, itself within a dream that never occurred. But, mark this and gather around, what you are about to see is only so much as our Creator allows.

Look! Look at our pair. How they duck beneath an archway proclaiming 'Nothing At All'. Yet seek to release every spirit He imprisoned for any want of an unchallenged whim. How she – how they – attempt to release you from Him, Whisperer, Thief. Taker of Brides.

How these colouring skies give warning. Gods and clouds forming beasts to devour every breath of scorched air. Here, dragons manoeuvre, furnace-belly supernova, explode and electrify. A show almighty for this melodramatic theatre of annulment.

And now, as our maidens retreat, the web patched and pieced, we must turn our attention in search of He; engrossed in the search for His estranged bride. So fixed in lost pursuit, unaware of those here requiring His presence.

Trillions look on. Every bride. And now – Creator.

This is all I have. It is everything that could ever have been. And now, my Lord, allow me leave. I have addressed you all, and with this, our first witness is required in attendance.'

And, without so much as a sideway step, our rook is aloft.

'(I leave you to reflect upon a wedding, but not all is as it seems)'

These blundering tides, disguised, wired and spliced, pull upon the orbit of a stencilled moon. And this inflating and deflating as if catching breath in the weighted run over a glazed and crayoned canvas. And all of this, and every kiss that might have set sail between horizons, groom and bride, dawn and an ebb tide evening heralding the night. The dust of the dead turn skies red and bluster and bolster and become breathtaking beasts. The locks that seized and promises whispered, not least, to beautiful brides, all twisted and tempered as suited to plumes and manes of running horses – yes, built from that dust of forgotten graves. And now new bones cracked and crushed settle their own dust, awaiting a draught to lift and gather into a cloud, blown up with the winds, then down onto an equally forgotten shore.

The ghosts tumble on, awaiting another call, rise from the earth, phased and formed from suns that neither turn nor burn and no longer seek out shadows. From ages and aeons before anything was born, drawn or feigned to move on beyond the moment. Everything in its place. Only the ghosts displaced. Nothing is nothing, yet is multiplied by one. Which zero is yin, and from what is yang?

Yes. These blustering tides divide the shores and swallow the dust claimed from those stars. Pull and they push, level and crush, decimate and devastate, fearing unheard collapse, back into that invisibled point of singularity.

No time?

No season?

No ascension.

(only the meaningless rotation of sterile universes)

All directions are signposted to 'Nothing At All'.

Arrival here affords no resolve.

Journeys from here evolve and subside, disintegrate and break with the tides.

This is how it is.

This arrival, however, also brings love.

'As promised, jury –

- Return to a church.'

Arms full of flowers, shakes her hair loose, rising church towers; sun spires, chimes ringing, confettied glades flickered and scattered, for today we are gathered as we unite bride and Groom. From this day forward to today admire destiny's desire – have and to hold, glistening gold, encircling ever onward. And, for those in keeping, assembled and beating pulse to the riddle of random, begin and began and opened a vein that might explain whereupon a dream might flow. And where to go? Free – to the sea and oceans and soft explosions that give rise to a pounding heart.

'Here we are. Gathered to join, that no man may put asunder. Muster and rally our force to each other, merge and bloom this special bride to the whispering Groom.'

'It isn't us He is marrying! It is Him and me.!'

Church bells jangling.

'Can't you see?'

Rhyming rhythms of softly spoken divisions divide the skies as a shadow wings across a slanted sun. And the congregation arise to offer a ring to slow the pain.

'No!'

'Man and wife.'

And immediately upon a train, freewilled for farewells.'

'No!'

'You belong to Me.'

'No!'

'I shall allow him life. But you must raise a toast to rest in peace. I shall decide. Am I not being fair? That you may cherish this last moment together? Can you not share this final instant of togetherness? Afterall – It was only a kiss.'

Red skies again.

As those horses assemble.

And the wolves pull upon their chains.

Gather and shape.

Goodbyes and refrains. Sad little things that could amount to something which means nothing at all.

'A kiss?'

'Nothing at all. Allow him to drop. You must catch the first mare. Will return you to Me. All destinies are Mine – in event you cannot see. There is nothing ever could alter so much as a flicker in a flame. There is no power in heaven

or hell could regain even a fraction of freedom.'

'Only the rivers.'

'Let him go. I need to know. The forces of the universe flow back upon themselves. Remember to take the mane of the very first mare. The others that follow ensure it is exact and blow dust to cover their tracks. Do it and be done! Chink glasses and be damned!'

'And the rook.'

And the jury continue to look on.

Here.
　　　Could this periphery of vision blur one edge or drive a wedge between a fate of twists that turn so vaguely? Could this indefinite momentum bring so much as a ruffle in the general emptiness of these hallowed halls. The souls have gone.

Here.

Abandoned.

Here.

Imagined images, perhaps?

Perhaps….but gone.

'Is this where you were when I could not find you? This unforsaken wilderness without light? Was it here you hid, in death, stopped as we leapt and hit the earth, deserted, yet hands still locked? Separated, pausing the clocks? Togethered, but untogethered, split between life and death? That is where we were – isolated and distanced and existence delayed in our hole behind a star. That is where we were. And this is where we are. We remember, yet restored to *somewhere* now, deep below our woods. Hairpinned time obliterating a shambled nightmare. The church and train – and now back again. We should be up there, released from our jar, waiting for the stars.'

'A short while, my love. All has become amiss.'

'I do not even know where we are.'

'It can be corrected with a kiss.'

'Then, kiss and let's be done.'

'He *is coming! Be quick!'*

E ntrance.
  Head already full of whispers.

Mantled darkness.

'Not so invisibled now!'

Lantern flicker.

'If you kiss her, all that is shall be undone; and all that is not, completely untied. Every precious bride, every screaming wraith, every bloodshot sky, offered as sacrifice as I reunite with my first and foremost bride – destiny. Ecstasy and pain. Encircled without circles. Squared, unrepaired and lost. How dare you remain! There is no redemption. I stand by my word.'

'Kiss me.'

If ever a kiss were a prayer.

If ever an embrace ever shared.

Were they able to stare.

Into one another's eyes.

Watching the world dissolve.

Away.

As the everyness of everything and everness rush colours into the grey, flooding the rivers, bursting the banks, rising over the high tides, over the boundaries and ramps, dancing lustres over the brimming wells, pouting, pouring and drawing and pulling and forming and calling silence to the bells of a church; merging, diverging, yet inert.

A touch of lips.

That is all.

Every universe spills nonchalantly away.

Every particle-cum-wave, entangled, fade and grade as one.

Yin into Yang.

Where it began.

And Yang into Yin.

Begin and reform.

Sunblinded.

A primeval dawn reawakens.

A touch of lips.

From this.

Our trillioned audience looks on.

Our forgotten brides.

'We are one in the sight of God.'

Our rook arrives. Usher, in fact. With a flutter of black and a rush in his eyes.

Side to side.

'Court in session. Your attendance and presence required.'

'Off Away! Back to thy waiting nest. These end of days desire no atonement. This end of grace. This embrace that withers away with the moment. Why should I attend? What defence should I offer? None to Him! I say. And, under what authority do these trillions gaze, amazed and open mouthed? By what charge or power are they released thus, to sway and prevail upon the outline of this vista?

'The creator becomes impatient.'

'Hah! And you would escort me to this juryless court?'

'Indeed! With dragons, in fact. Your horses have already fled.'

Side to side.

Pauses.

'Creator awaits.'

'Indeed.'

I **am brought before you.**
Now – Back to rest, or off to wherever from here! There must be other areas of business more demanding of your attention. Other – far, faraway – existences requiring specific intervention. Not here! My sleepy little web requires no more than minor corrections, that is all.

How a kiss could rouse your diversion?
From where so remote?
It is of no interest to Me.
I create illusion and war. Too far from here
this heaven of yours.

Behold!
Alpha, yet Omega – Beginning to end.
From such a height to fall!
Crashing upon your door.
And the crying aloud of the myriads more.
The first seal of seven expects.
These horses ridden by death.
This sun blackens as the moon blood reds. The stars
are falling to earth.
Chariots prepare for battle, awaiting the seventh seal.
A dragon steals, stirring because time runs short.
No bride here.
No bridegroom.
Only the key to the great abyss.

'Alas! It was not the kiss that awoke me.'

'Twinkle, twinkle, every solitary star, every myopic
moon and balustrade running parallel to the dim

haze of indistinct shadows and shallows and narrow hide and seeks. Every soul's incarnation meets upon another. Every spirit that wandered, lost and alone, hushed and gathered, mirror-shattered and scattered a trillion shards. Every shiver, fragment and splinter. Every tiniest piece, atom to infinity, reflection and mimicry echoing back strange mutation. Tinted and smogged, every sigh that breathed upon the glass could not maintain anonymity. This abstracted cubist symmetry changes with every breath, every life and death, no more and no less.

Every spirit gather around. See how these pieces reflect back one into each other as cards turn and the web shudders and the heavens and hells and wells flood and cover every one, every other, every sacrifice raised to the face of God. And as the pendulum keeps count, one coming in, and one going out, the totals are tallied and tallied again, balanced on account of one and the same. All things must pass, yet remain unchanged. All things exactly correct and true. All those universes fragile and thin, sparkling in the darkness, reaper hooded and reaper grim, black holes spinning back to beginning and critical mass; yet these, like our hosts, are entangled, too. I say this; for all I have seen and onto each its own tower per collection, every tiniest piece locks one breath upon the promise of resurrection.

I say this also; neither *this* I am, nor *that*; neither either, *either*, or. Witness, yes. Usher, yes. Mediator, nothing more. For, as you know, I am free. As are the rivers that run below me. Yet not the moon over which I glide, or the stars, or the holes behind which some hide – following the flaws of the web and He.

I say this finally; I observe and *pre*serve, I know nothing of anything – except witness to bear. And were it for me to decide, I would allow kisses also to be free. However, permit exception.

But now, here gathering, last two witnesses to be called.

Bated breath.'

S piral stair ascending, these two sharing every footstep back up to door and wood where circles turn as they should and rooks alight from midway nests, and thunderstorms arrive, and skies redden and absorb. They pour upon prelude to desire. They soak and spray, as though every delay might lose even a molecule of passion. They fury, yet abate, separate and open to starry skies. The starry-eyed look toward heaven. And, at once, conceivably dreaming throughout the climb, arrive at the highest door.

There are no locks here.

Door allowed to open.

Gentle push.

'We are here?'

'No. Somewhere else.'

'Where are the woods? Have we become lost?'

Opening and arrival of light.

'I know where we are.'

'How do you know this?'

'We have your ally.'

'Step forward!' calls a voice. 'Court in session.'

'**A**ll present and correct!'
The swirl and murmuration of energies dance as one – as a totality whilst the circle completes.

In that finite instant the moment sees itself; a drop suspended in the invisibled point of singularity whereupon every atom locks into every atom, every tip of every dimension touches, every moment becomes meaningless and *everness* twists into *uneverness*.

'We are gathered oblique, out-of-focus, out of time, four corners wherein crushed flowers, skeletal leaves, and random death are rushed as if by hurricanes into any haven.

The background noise merely a trivial frenzy offering no sanctuary. It convulses abracadabra equations and adds them together, final zero.

Order to disorder.

My will be done.

Because we are *all* entangled.'

Upon which corner do these dead collect? Upon which illusion would you deem to forget? Upon what, or which, or whatever whenever would these together amount to anything more than this?

Come on!

I oversee this web. This playground of infinite themes dreaming ridiculous ploys. These voids unfilled, these halls *my* will. And since when, of late, do you ever allow a second thought?

Back to sleep, I say. Back turned. Back to

wherever your *evers* might be. They are not here.. Elsewhere. Wherever, in deed, you should be.

Leave us.

Would you have us become soft waves ebbing against your shore? Would you have us dilly-dally in whispers for evermore? Would you? Would you ask that we pray, repent and to stay – because far, far away, one day, thy will be done, and thy kingdom prevail?

I have nothing else to say.'

So it is and sobeit, then – the prophesies completely wronged, overturned and unbelonged to these saturnine, sable days.

So it is, or so they say – these prophesies I pray delayed no longer. These heresies territories of yours and mine divide divine – where is there compromise to offer? And when?

Run a finger over the seventh seal. Muster the armies to ready. This is not the time that is no time. Not yet. The dance continues.

I bid our lovers speak.'

(In whispers) *'Of what should we speak?'*
'And to whom do we address? (below breath) Are

we required to repent? And to which party does that rook represent?'

'All parties, of course. He is of whom I spoke.'

'Your friend?'

Our friend. Deliverance and Hope. Witness to all things. Arbitrator and balancer and proprietor of every existence and equidistance scattered or via gathered collection.

'Of what should we say whilst they wait upon us?'

'Nothing. There is nothing to say.'

Then, come into my arms and hold me forever. Seal my lips with a kiss – never let go. Seal our hearts for all this is all we keep and all we would wish or ever dream to know.'

(sighs)

'– Kiss –'

'Words indeed – when, in deed, words fail. The oceans run away as we prepare and ready to sail. The skies turn upon a spirit-levelled horizon where hides a rising evening veil. All the reds sputter and falter as each opposing world awaits upon an alter where offerings are hurriedly sourced. Yet here a kiss! Treasure this! Reveal it to every broken heart. It was never, however, the first kiss that awoke me, but the softest flutter of little wings captured in a jar.

You are free to return; wedding, by dragons, annulled. Released from the web vice-versal, begin and rebegin – your circle awaits. A gift from our friend who will oversee your return.'

(a nod –and side-to-side)

'But there is one thing you must do……'

Fly with me by way of all this. There are now two new stars in the sky. Glide with me back to begin, back before to dance.

Feel this headrush as the web retightens without you. Discharged, beyond done and undone. Liberated. The clocks that were stopped are all chiming now. Their pendulums and cogs ticking for someone. The dust disturbed has settled again. And the rivers and drains flow straight to the sea. And the dead await life, queued in line, unaware of any such measure of time, queued for their entrance, queued for their play in this little pantomime.

It is almost done.

And at the count of Three…..

One.

Two.

And…..

Three (all undone).

Gathered and we are gathered.

Unified and absolute.

Those armies pause and raise a toast to their ghosts enroute.

Arrived.

'Circle by a tree! Quickly! With me!'

'Where are we going? And running to where? And – Have we really awoken from there?'

'To set a spirit free.'

A rook alights upon a bough. Over a circle drawn in the ground.

'No dream!'
'Exactly where we left her!'
(a flutter of butterfly wings)
'Hurry on over!'
'Lift her and set her free!'
Butterfly away.
'Now – Take my hand…'
(kiss)

And up and upon and beyond all of this, underscored orchestras swell and lift tuneless tides to faraway shores.

Away

And

Away.

The incomplete circle completes.

The indistinct brides return to sleep.

Whilst rook and butterfly resume their tempo of random ascent, partakers and collators of this and every entanglement and whisper ever lost to love. Their roles unfolding so much as might freedom allow. And the quick and the dead and those released from the web

Adding two new

Additions

To the twilight collage.

Reconfigurate.

One-hundred-and-fifty-eight

Stars

In

A

Farewell

Sky.